A SAVAGE LOVE SO DEADLY

BY: BARBIE AMOR

*AUTHOR FORMALLY KNOWN
AS "BARBIE SCOTT"*

D1519367

*THIS IS A WORK OF FICTION. ALL
OF THE CHARACTERS, ORGANIZA-*

PROLOGUE

"**O**h my Goddd. Please!"

I jumped out my sleep to the sound of my mother's screams. It was something about the way she sounded that petrified me. I tried hard to listen, and the more I heard her screaming, the more my insides cringed. I was scared to get out of my bed but I had to see what was wrong with my mom. My dad was at work which made me more nervous than I already was. I cursed myself because I had taken the cordless phone into the living room after talking to this chick for hours.

I climbed out of my bed and peeked my head out my bedroom door. It was pitch black and the only sound that could be heard was my mother's screams and cries. Creeping down the hall, I made it to my mother's bedroom door.

"Why are you doing this to me! Please god nooo!" she was crying. I could hear tussling and suddenly the sound of a slap made me stop in my tracks. When I peeked into my mother's room, she was holding her face as she sobbed. The man standing over her wore a mask and he began hitting repeatedly.

Creek

The sound of the door creekin made them both look over. I was so scared I began to back away from the door. "Blessing run!" my mother screamed out. As I backed up down the hall, the mask man came rushing in my direction. "Blessing run baby!" the more my mother screamed the more scared I became.

"You little bastard." the man said and knocked me to the ground. It was something familiar about his voice but the ski mask muffled his full sound. My eyes grew wide, as I watched him pull out his gun. Using my elbows to scoot backwards, he fired a shot into my stomach.

"Ahhhhh!" I screamed and grabbed my bullet wound.

"You bastard!" my mom charged at him. He back hand her knocking her to the ground. He then walked over to her and stood over her as she screamed. Without warning he scooped her up and tossed her over his shoulder. I thought he was gonna take her back into her room then this would give me a chance to call my dad. Instead, he carried her out the door.

I used all the energy I had to stand to my feet. I was bleeding so bad my shirt and now pajamas were covered in blood. I staggered to the door to make sure this muthafucka didn't harm my mother but I was too late. He had slammed her into his car and sped down the block with her screaming. Tears began to pour from my eyes and next thing I know, I passed out.

CHAPTER 1

Blessing

"Bless! Bless!" my boy Echo screamed my name bringing me from my daze.

"Huh. My bad foo?"

"My nigga. You was in a straight daze. You good?"

"Yeah I'm good." I lied. I wasn't good. I was in a daze thinking bout my moms. I thought of her all year long but every time around this year, I thought of that day.

Thanksgiving day was the day I was shot and my mother was taken from me. It's been 13 years and every day this shit bothered me. I really hated Thanksgiving. I mean, what did I really have to be thankful for? My mother was taken out of my life on this day. All these years and not a trace of her. We put out missing reports and even a huge *Have you seen me* billboards in surrounding states. My father had his friends from the military do a on foot manhunt and still nothing.

The night my mom was taken, my neighbor was the one who found me lying in a pool of my own blood. I was rushed to the hospital and had to have a blood transfusion. Until this day, I wore the scare but fuck the scar, I wanted my mother back. For many years, I had nightmares about that night and every time I woke up, I wished it was just a dream. However, reality would always hit me; this shit was real. So to me, Thanksgiving was just another day, and I would spend it in my crib drinking until I couldn't walk.

"I hope this nigga here." Echo said, making me search the lot for Rolo's whip.

We were at the car dealership because Echo wanted to cop a new whip. Rolo was my plug so I was the one that could get a car for him with a few thousand knocked off.

"I hope he is too. I might cop that new Bent truck if they got it."

"Yeah, that muthafucka clean."

"Let's roll up in here." I told him and we exited the whip.

When we walked inside, Lameka was at the front desk and I was now pissed because I wasn't trying to be bothered with her right now. Lameka was my girl of two years who always had her hand out. I didn't mind spending on her but the bitch was hella money hungry. No matter what I did for her it was never enough. We had a fat ass crib, she had plenty cars to drive and a closet that was phat with tags still hanging on fifty percent of the shit. I had met Lameka through my girl cousin Poodie. She was only supposed to be a fuck but because she was around all the time, we fucked on a regular. She pretty much made herself my girl. Because she was bad as hell, I didn't mind having her on my arms. But now, I regretted it.

"We not hiring. Do you not understand English."

"I don't understand why I can't talk to a manager."

"I just told yo simple ass I was the manager. And we're not hiring." Lameka told some chick who was at her desk. The chick was dressed simple but she had a pretty ass face. She looked upset, and I couldn't blame her. The way Meka was talking to her would have anybody tripping. Lameka was cocky as fuck and since she been hired she was feeling herself. Tired of her spending my money I had Rolo plug her with the job but this shit didn't work. Every time I looked up my credit card statements were through the roof.

Frustrated with Lamkea the girl turned around to leave

bumping right into me.

"Excuse me." she looked up at me through a pair of innocent eyes. This girl was pretty as fuck.

"You good." I told her but she didn't move. Instead, she stared at me and I stared right back. She had the most beautiful eyes I'd ever seen. They weren't colored or anything but they were almond shaped and big like a Walt Disney princess.

"Hey baby." Lameka said letting it be known I belonged to her. The chick looked back embarrassed then back to me. She then stormed out making sure to let the door slam.

"Where Rolo?"

"Damn, hi to you too."

"I'm not in the mood right now Meka."

"You ain't never in the mood."

I ignored her and waited for her to page Rolo.

When Rolo walked in, he dapped me and Echo then pulled us to the floor.

"What you trying to get Echo?"

"A Porsche. what you got for me?"

"I got the 911."

"Run it." Echo said without seeing the car. He was smiling hard and rubbing his hands together.

"Oh yeah. Wrap this bitch up." I told Rolo walking over to a red Bentley truck.

"I hope you buying me a new car." We all turned around to Lameka nosey ass. I couldn't do shit but shake my head at her.

"Get back to work Meka." Rolo said, noticing I was getting irate. She rolled her eyes and walked back over to the front desk. "Your uncle came and buy Mercedes two days ago."

"Man, fuck that weird ass nigga." I told him and meant every word.

My uncle Marshon was what anyone would refer to as weird. The way he acted and even the way he talked. The nigga was a six foot creep and I was happy he had moved to Tallahassee.

Uncle Marshon had went and done fourteen years in jail for

rape. It's been fourteen years since he's been home but I swear, jail did something to that nigga. My pops didn't fuck with him and I for damn sure didn't fuck with his hating ass. Every time he came to visit for the holidays, he always had some slick shit to say. He would always say shit about me selling dope and that shit pissed me off. Nigga had his fucking nerves. I could remember a time when we had an argument and the nigga picked me up off my feet and pinned me against the wall. I was seventeen and by the grace of God, my father had walked through the door. Him and my uncle started fist fighting blow for blow until they were both tired. After that day, I told myself I was gonna murk that nigga. I was young then but I swear if he tried that shit now, he'd be dead and his body would be floating in the Bayou. My pops always told me let it go but fuck that; one day, that nigga was gonna meet the barrel of my gun.

"Start the paperwork and run them keys." I looked up at Rolo. It was time to roll because I had shit to do. I had to go cook my work and drop it off to my trap. And not to mention my Pops was throwing a family meeting tonight and I couldn't be late. These family meetings were important to my pops and step moms. Although I hated them I tried to be supportive.

CHAPTER 2

Cherish

I was standing up at the front of the bus holding onto the railing. I stood in front of Miracle who was sitting down and had now dozed off. Every five minutes I looked down at my watch cursing under my breath. The dumbass driver stopped at every stop and the bus was already to capacity.

Finally coming up to our stop, I pulled the cord to ring the bell. When the bus stopped I grabbed Miracle and pulled her into my arms. Getting off the bus, I shook her awake because we had about six blocks to walk. My poor baby was tired as hell but we had to get going. I grabbed her hand and pulled her up the street. After about fifteen minutes, we had finally arrived and I was out of breath.

"You're ten minutes late."

"I was out job hunting."

"I'm sorry; I can't let you in."

"But I was job hunting. Please Danny."

"Sorry, I can't do it."

My eyes began to weld up with tears but I refused to cry in front of this nigga.

"You just mad I won't fuck your fat ass." I told him then stormed away.

"Ohh, mommy you said a bad word." Miracle giggled.

"I'm sorry baby." I apologized embarrassed. I never cursed in front of my baby but right now I was upset.

"Where we going mommy?"

"I don't know baby." I replied to her sadly.

As we walked up the street, we were passing by a Walmart. We headed inside and went to the linen section. I grabbed a king size blanket that was inside of a clear packaging and we made our way to the counter. I walked past each check-out counter trying to analyze which register was clear. "Come on Miracle." I pulled her hand as we sped past the counter. Everyone was occupied with customers so we made a dash for the door. Walking out of the door, I let out a breath I had been holding since walking in. We were safe and sound and now my concern was where the hell were we going to sleep.

***

After laying the blanket down, Miracle and I laid down inside of it. I pulled the cover over us making sure to keep warm. I knew I wouldn't be able to sleep because of the headlights that drove by every minute. It was a bit chilly out, so I made sure to put Miracle on the inside. Tears began to fall from my eyes as I thought of how this had become my life. Me and my five-year-old daughter were on the side of a freeway, wrapped up in a blanket I had just stolen. I had no friends and thanks to my child's father I had no family.

I had met Paul when I was nineteen. The first time I saw him, it was love at first sight. He did everything in the book to get me, and with his charm he won me over. He was the nicest guy and he catered to my every need. He was handsome and rolling in dough and he used his money to manipulate me. He could do no wrong in my eyes; until, after the first six months he had begun to turn into the real him. All the charming and catering was bullshit and I soon found out. He had become possessive and basically held me captive. He moved us to New Orleans just to get me away from my family. I was so in love, my dumbass came and regretted it shortly after.

A few months after moving, he began cheating and started

treating me like shit. When I called him out on it he would deny it. He eventually found a girl he liked because when I confronted him the second time, his response was *so*. I couldn't believe my ears. I ran to our bedroom and packed my things. I was five months pregnant by this time but I didn't care. I was leaving him; or so I thought. He came into the room and beat my ass until I was unconscious. Then had the nerve to wake me up and heal my wombs. He told me he loved me and I fell for it.

I stayed around for another three years dealing with heartache and abuse. He was the best father ever but he was on the worst boyfriend list. Not being able to take it anymore, I built up enough courage to leave him. I went to the county to apply as homeless and they put me into a hotel for three weeks. I thought I had escaped my reality but I failed. Paul found me and beat my ass until he broke my nose and blacked both my eyes. My screams alerted the motel staff and they called the police. Paul went to jail and they gave his ass only two years. Two fucking years and he had damn near killed me. Once he got locked away, I was left with nothing. I moved into my friend's house and things were cool for about a year. When her boyfriend was released from jail she started acting funny so I took it upon myself to leave. We were bumping heads over the smallest things. The last straw was when she called herself whooping my daughter. I beat her ass until she threatened to call the police on me so I left. And that's how I ended up here.

Right now, I was living in a shelter and I been here for four months. Every day I searched for a job but I didn't have any luck. I had about another two months before I qualified for low income so I was trying my best to hold tight. Whenever I was late, the shelter the security wouldn't let me in. Just like tonight. I was only ten minutes late and Danny rejected my entrance. I knew it was because I wouldn't sleep with his fat ass. So here I was, on the side of the freeway with my child nestled close to me. I was mad as hell because I was gonna have to go to the shelter in the morning to get Miracle ready for school which would be extremely hard to do.

11

"Mommy it's cold." she said and I could see her teeth shaking.

"I'm sorry baby." I replied and pulled her close to me. I pulled the blanket all the way over us and said a silent prayer. We only had to deal with this for a couple more months and I couldn't wait until it was over.

***

The next morning, I took Miracle to school and headed back to the shelter. When I walked in, the staff was hanging decorations on the wall. We were a month from Thanksgiving and I was starting to feel sad. I began to think about the times when I would be with my family pigging out and enjoying Hennessy and eggnog. When my grandmother was alive was when things were peachy. The moment she passed my family began to separate. That's when I met Paul. My mother and I haven't spoken since because she hated that man. After Paul had gone to jail, I called her to ask if I could come back home. I explained to her how Paul was now incarcerated and she had the nerves to say, oh you calling me now. I hung up on her and never called her again.

"I can't wait to eat some turkey."

I turned around and Cherry was admiring the decor.

"Yeah, me either." I lied with a faint smile.

"Don't look like that Cherish. This shit gonna be over soon." she said and rubbed my shoulder.

Cherry was a chick I had met inside the shelter. We both had similar situations except she actually killed her child father. She had done seven years behind bars and pretty much came home to nothing. Cherry was pretty cool. She was actually the only chick I talked to in the facility. She on the other hand had more friends inside, but I wasn't in the position to make friends. After dealing with Verlin, someone who I considered a friend, the word friendship left a bad taste in my mouth.

"I overheard Camille talking about some guy named Blessing who is coming to serve. Whoever he is, she is head over heels in love with him."

"That don't surprise me. That hoe in love with everybody."

"You're so crazy." Cherry laughed. "You right though. Shit she slept with Morgan and Trevor." She said referring to the male staff members.

"She probably slept with Danny too." we both laughed. Camille was what people would call a hater. She didn't know me from a can of paint but she hated my guts. I couldn't understand for the life of me why because she had it all. A great job, a nice car, her own house and she dressed nice.

"That bitch wanna be you so bad." Cherry said looking over in her direction. Just the sight of her made my insides cringe.

"I don't know why, I ain't got shit. Bitch just weird man."

Cherry and I headed over to the breakfast table and made our plate. We took a seat in the cafeteria and began to chat. This was gonna be our spot until it was time to pick up Miracle from school. I was so pooped from yesterday, I didn't bother to go job hunting today. I was gonna lay down and watch me some TV.

CHAPTER 3

Blessing

Walking into my Pop's crib, I knew he was gonna chew me out for being late. The first face I saw was my cousin Poodie and of course her miserable ass called me out on my tardiness.

"Uncle Mike, he's finally here." she said screaming for my dad.

"Shut yo hating ass up."

"Owell, yo ass should have been on time. You always act like you a damn Prince and we gotta wait on you."

"Man, shut the fuck up Poodie damn. A nigga already not in the mood for this shit." I mugged her.

"Leave him the fuck alone hoe. You know he already hates this time of year." my cousin Shani said backing me up.

"And you always captain saving this nigga. Mind yo business."

"I'll mind mine when you mind yours hating ass bitch." Shani said now getting upset. Poodie didn't want it with Shani from the hands. Her ass was all mouth. As kids they stayed fighting and Shani would always beat her ass. Poodie was the cousin from hell that always talked shit. I couldn't understand why because her jobless ass didn't have a pot to piss in and damn sure no window to toss it from. Which was the reason she was living with my Pops and step moms. Lazy ass couldn't take the rules at her mom's crib so she left.

"Hello son?' my step mother smiled as she walked into the dining room. She was holding a pan of food that she sat down before coming over to hug me.

My step moms Evelyn was cool as shit. She loved me like I was her own, and I actually enjoyed having her. My pops had pretty much fallen into depression after my mother went missing. He wouldn't date, shit he barely went outside. Seven years had gone by and finally he met Evelyn. Within two years they had married and she had been around ever since.

"Son, why the hell you late?" my father said now coming into the dinner room.

"I had shit to do dad."

"Boy, watch yo mouth." my step mother looked over at me.

"My bad." I chuckled.

"Well, I'm glad you're here. Now we can go on with our meeting."

"Yes, your Prince is here, can we start." Poodie rolled her eyes.

"Bitch, keep talking and I'mma have Shani beat yo ass." Out of the side of my eye, I could feel Shani's smile. All I had to do was say get her and believe you me, Poodie would be laid the fuck out.

"Boy, watch yo damn mouth calling that girl out her name."

"Fuck her. Now can we start this meeting so I can roll. I got shit to do."

"Blessing!" again my step mother said.

"With all due respect moms, I'm a grown ass man. Pops curse like a sailor." she looked at me shocked that I had spoken to her in such a manner but I didn't give a fuck; I'm grown.

"Look, y'all know I don't give a fuck about this bullshit holiday. I'm only doing it for y'all."

"You watch your damn mouth boy." my father shot with base in his voice. I sighed and sat back in my seat.

"Now son, I know you're still hurt about what happened but

you have a lot to be thankful for."

"Material shit ain't gone bring my mother back dad."

"True, but you're alive and you're healthy." he looked at me and I could see the hurt in his eyes. I know I was being an ass but I was tired of this shit every year. I didn't understand why I couldn't just grieve to myself every year. Instead, I had to be in the Thanksgiving spirit. Not only did I have to worry about the day coming up, but I had to tag along and go to the shelter to feed the homeless. Everything about that place made me hate the day more. They would have all these damn decorations on the walls and even the staff dressed up like pilgrims. I didn't mind feeding the homeless any other day. I mean, we always did shit in the hood for the kids and the community. I just wasn't feeling this day but I had to do it so I wouldn't seem like the Grinch.

"When we going? What time and what should I bring?"

"This Saturday, 9:00am and bring some turkeys. If you don't mind."

"You know I don't mind." I hit my step mom with a head nod. When she smiled, I smiled and now I was more relaxed.

"Son, don't bring all them damn turkeys again." my Pops said, making everybody laugh. I nodded my head ok because I was sure gonna do it. Last time we fed the homeless they put me in charge of the turkeys. I had so many I had to rent a van to load them. Shit how was I supposed to know how many we needed. I figured two hundred would be enough but I guess I overdid it. We always went in to feed the homeless three weeks before and because of all the turkeys we went back again the day before the holiday.

"Aight, can I leave now?" I asked, looking at my Pops.

"You're not staying for dinner?" he asked shocked. I always came over to eat dinner but Meka was at my crib cooking.

"Naw. Meka cooking." I replied standing to my feet. When my Pops gave me a head nod of approval, I left and hopped in my whip. I contemplated just hitting up the club because I really didn't want to see Meka right now. Deciding to just go home, I

16

headed for the highway and went home.

**

I opened my eyes and looked over at the clock. It was a little after six so I tapped Meka so she could start getting ready. It literally took this girl two hours to get dressed so I had to wake her up hours before. When she woke up the first thing she did was grab my dick. I shook my head because this all she ever wanted to do. Don't get me wrong, I love pussy. It was just her I was getting tired of.

"Man, go get ready." I told her and lifted out the bed.

"Okay." she sighed and lifted up. She stumbled into the restroom and turned on the shower. I headed in behind her so I could handle my hygiene.

"You not gone shower with me?"

"Nah, I gotta go cook my work real quick." I told her. She thought she was slick. All she was trying to do was get me to fuck her in the shower but I wasn't falling for it. I quickly brushed my teeth then headed into the kitchen.

Once I was done cooking my work, I went to take a quick shower. After I was done I slid on some grey sweats and a fresh white tee. I kept it simple with my jewelry only throwing on my rope chain and Jesus piece. Not feeling like brushing my waves, I grabbed my black Raiders cap and sat it on my head. By the time I was done, Meka had just finished. I shook my head at her slow ass and made my way for the door.

By the time we pulled up to the shelter, Echo was pulling up with the turkeys. I climbed out and began helping him take them in. Instead of cooking them I brought them already cooked which was a good idea because they cooked them and wrapped them in pans. After we were done unloading, we headed inside to help serve.

Standing behind the table, I was in charge of cutting the

turkey and putting it on the plates. There was a long ass line so I knew this would be a long ass day. I cut the first turkey and placed it on the plate then passed it to Meka who was in charge of putting the sides on the plates. Shani was on the opposite side of the table greeting the people, and my Pops and moms were in charge of serving.

"Aww she's so pretty." Shani cooed at a little girl who appeared to be about four or five. She was a cute little girl. The fact that she was in this shelter made me look up to see who she belonged to and my eyes fell on to the same chick I had seen in the dealership.

"Thank you," she smiled at Shani. When she walked up to the head of the line, she looked up at me and our eyes connected. She brushed a strand of hair from her face and put her head down embarrassed. *Damn baby girl living in here?* I thought as I watched her. When she walked away from the table I couldn't take my eyes off her. Despite the clothing she wore and her hair not fresh from a shop, she was pretty as a muthafucka. I ain't gone lie, she had a nigga intrigued. I wondered what was her story and how she ended up here.

Shani grabbed the little girl's plate and followed her mother over to the table. As soon as she sat down, she looked back over to me and I was still looking at her.

"Eww. Shani talks to anybody." Meka said, looking at Shani and the chick.

"You saying ewww like she got cooties or something."

"I'm sure she is living here. Do you see her clothing? And trying to be cute. How you cute in a shelter." Meka said and laughed at her own joke. I didn't see shit funny so I was about to humble her ass.

"You would be living here if I didn't get you off the streets. Meka you ain't no better than the next chick. You got a roof over your head thanks to me and let's not forget that job you got is because of me. Humble yourself ma because as fast as you got it, you could lose it." I told her and turned to feed the next person in line.

For the rest of our serving, Meka had an attitude which was fine with me. I didn't have to talk to her because I didn't kiss ass. Especially, her ass. Every now and then I would look over at the table fascinated by the chick. Shani was still at her table and her mouth was moving a mile a minute.

"Hi I'm Camille." some chick walked over to introduce herself. By the way she was dressed I figured she worked here instead of living here. "I'm the staff coordinator." she smiled and reached her hand out for me to shake. I looked at her as if she had shit on her hands so she quickly moved it back.

"And you're telling me this why?" I asked, making her frown up. Instead of her replying, she walked off and went over to the side to talk to someone. I shook my head and laughed.

"Shani a fucking bum magnet." I heard the most annoying voice ever. I didn't even have to look up to know it was Poodie. Meka went to laugh and when I shot her an evil look she stopped. I swear these two bitches wasn't shit. I couldn't wait until this shit was over to get away from them. I already didn't want to be here and they were dampening my damn mood.

CHAPTER 4

Blessing

"**A**ye cuzzo I'm out." I walked over to where ol girl and Shani sat talking.

"Y'all done already?" she asked looking around.

"Yeah, yo ass just done made you a new friend you forgot about us." I said but not once taking my eyes off the chick.

"My bad cousin." she giggled. When she noticed I kept looking at ol girl she took it upon herself to introduce us.

"Blessing, this is Cherish. Cherish, this is my handsome and half single cousin Blessing." she laughed.

"Half single?" I laughed along with them.

"How you doing, Cherish?" I nodded to her then looked back to Shani.

"I'm Miracle." the pretty little girl that sat next to her said, making us all smile.

"How are you doing? I'm Blessing." I extended my hand for her to shake.

"Blessing." she repeated then giggled. She then looked back down to her coloring book so I turned back to Shani. "I'm out so hit me." I told her then turned to leave. Before I could walk away, I had to get one more glance at Cherish. She had a set of big pretty brown eyes that lit up under the lighting. Her lips were perfect with the dent at the top. Her smile was the beautifulist I'd ever seen and she had some pretty white teeth. Her hair was a little past her shoulders and she wore it down. I couldn't tell you what her body was like because she was overdressed but it really didn't matter because her smile alone had a nigga.

When I stepped out into the air, the sun was still bright but it was a little chilly. I walked towards my truck and just when I was about to hop in someone called my name. I turned around to see the same chick that worked inside the facility. I stood there because if the bitch wanted me, she had to come to me. Noticing I wasn't moving, she walked her thirsty ass over to me. I was glad I had sent Meka with Poodie because there would have been a fight.

"Hey umm...I just wanted to say thank you."

"You're welcome." I replied then turned to leave.

"I ummm...had been trying to get in touch with you for months now. I wanted to speak with you about the fundraiser you were having coming up." I knew this bitch was lying because we hadn't even scheduled a date. We had fundraisers every year but like I said we didn't even know when.

"Look ma, if you wanna fuck a nigga just say it. All this lying and shit ain't called for." I turned back around to face her.

"I'm sorry. I just didn't know what to say."

"Here, take my number because I gotta roll." she quickly reached into her side pocket of her vest and pulled out her phone.

"What's the number?" she eagerly asked as if I would change my mind. I read the number off to her then turned to leave. I watched her as I was pulling off and she was punching away on her keyboard. Moments later, a text came through my phone and for some reason I figured it was her.

Unknown number: I hope I could see you soon

I didn't bother to reply. I dropped my phone back into my passenger seat and headed for my trap. I wasn't worried about no pussy right now because a nigga had plenty. True, I had a bitch, but that didn't mean I wasn't bending nothing over outside of my home. I didn't see a future with Meka which was the reason she had her own crib. Until I found a bitch to make me happy then I would continue to do me.

***

Cherish

I laid in my cot and I couldn't get Blessing off my mind for the life of me. I wasn't normally attracted to his kind but it was something about him that had me interested. Not only was he handsome but I could also tell he was a kingpin of some sort. The way he moved he demanded the presence of anyone who was in his presence. Just the thought of his pretty bronze skin and perfect teeth made me clamp my legs tight to stop the throbbing between my center piece. He had a pair of eyes that were mysterious with a hint of sadness. He had full lips and underneath his right eye was a teardrop tattoo that made him sexier. I could also tell his body was covered in tattoos because I was sure he didn't just have his arms tatted. Underneath his hat I could tell he wore waves that were deeper than the Atlantic ocean. *Blessing.* I said his name to myself as I smiled. His name fit him perfectly because he was indeed a Blessing.

His cousin Shani was really nice to me today, and I could tell she was genuine. I didn't have a phone so she gave me her number. She also invited me over for dinner to her aunt's house where she said she spent most of her time. I didn't want to seem uppity so I agreed to come. I just hoped like hell I didn't run into Blessing because that man was intimidating.

"What you reading?"
"Loves Pain Within the Game."
"Ohh, who's that by?"
"Nique. It's pretty good too."
"I'mma have to read that when you're done."
"You're done with that other book?"
"Girl yes. I read that in four hours. Myss Shan books are sooo

good."

"What you reading now?" I asked her noticing she was holding a yellowish pink book I had never seen.

"The Real Dope Boyz of South Central."

"I wanna read it."

"Girl boo. You wouldn't know what to do with a dope boy."

"Girl please I'll blow a dope boyz mind." we both laughed. Cherry knew I was blowing smoke. I mean, I grew up around Dope Boyz; they just weren't my preference.

"Yeah, well that Dope Boy you were lusting over gone blow yo little mind and have you in the hood looking for his ass." I burst out laughing because her nosey ass had saw me eyeing Blessing. She had been cracking jokes about it every time we crossed paths all day. "You really like him huh?" she asked watching me.

"I don't even know him."

"Girl, it's written all over your face. Just the way you were looking at him today told it all. And then his ass gone try to act like he wanted to talk to his cousin. Nigga checking for you too."

"Nah, he has a half girlfriend."

"Huh?" she asked as I laughed.

"Nothing girl." I told her still laughing.

It's like the more Cherry talked about Blessing the more I thought of him. I don't know why but today he looked so sad. It was something in his eyes I couldn't read. The way he looked at the decorations was like he was reliving something. The entire time he didn't crack a smile until he came over and talked to Miracle. I sighed just thinking bout him and was now ready to call it a night. I knew he was gonna invade my dreams and I really didn't mind. This would probably be my first and only time ever seeing him so I was gonna try my hardest to shake these thoughts. I mean what would he do with a chick like me? I didn't have a job, a car, and my living condition was horrible. I'm sure to get on my feet soon but by the time that happened, it would be too late. *Sigh.*

***

The next morning, I woke up tired as ever. I reluctantly climbed out of my cot to go use the restroom. I looked over to a sleeping Miracle and I didn't want to wake her because she looked so peaceful. One thing I didn't do was ever leave my baby alone. I shook her lightly and she lifted up rubbing her eyes. I pulled her into my arms and headed for the ladies' room. I quickly used the restroom then washed my hands and headed out. On our way to the cot, I ran into Camille who instantly mugged. I rolled my eyes at her because it was too damn early for her bullshit. I swear this chick had it out for me for no damn reason. Yesterday, after she seen Blessing walk over to my table she had been mugging me something serious. Remembering what Cherry had said about her excited about him coming now I understood why. However, she had made a complete fool of herself because when she went over to talk to him. He looked annoyed by her presence. I watched as she tried to shake his hand and he declined. I wanted to laugh so bad but I didn't need the extra drama she came with.

Instead of getting back in bed, I went to see if Cherry was still asleep. When I neared her cot, I couldn't help but laugh. She had her night lamp on and was glued to her book. She looked up at me then down to Miracle.

"Come here baby." she said pulling Miracle into the bed with her. She scooted over and let her lay down. I could tell Miracle was gonna go back to sleep so I pulled the extra throw blanket Cherry had on her to cover her up.

"What's bothering you?" Cherry asked closing her book.

"I had to pee." I giggled.

"Other than that miss thang? Let me find out that boy on your mind." she smirked at me.

"I'm not thinking bout him. And I'm sure he's not thinking bout me. That man has a girl and I'm homeless. I mean did you

24

see her? She's beautiful and looked very well kept." I replied sadly.

"You don't know that. So what you're in this situation. Maybe he could tell you're a good person. Maybe he sees something in you. And so what she's pretty; you are too. I bet my last nine dollars she's well-kept because of him."

"Thank you." I beamed because she called me pretty. For so many years Paul tore down my self-esteem. He called me ugly and would always say, nobody would ever want yo ugly ass and I'mma make sure of it. Which was why he constantly blacked my eyes. For a moment I thought they would be permanent because it took years for the dark rings to go away.

"So are you gonna go?" she's asked knocking me from my thoughts.

"Where?"

"To the dinner his cousin invited you to."

"I don't know?"

"I think you should. You need to get out of this place and enjoy yourself. Have you a couple drinks and eat some home cooked food." she said then flipped back open her book. I thought about it for a minute but I decided not to go. *I'll deal with Shani when I get on my feet.* I thought. *Ugh.*

CHAPTER 5

Blessing

For three days I thought about Cherish. I don't know what it was but it was something about this chick. Her innocence alone made me see she was more than some gold digging bitch that wanted a nigga for his paypa. I saw it all in her eyes she wanted me but the vibe felt different. Her shy-like demeanor had me wanting to give her the confidence she needed. I could tell she was broken, and so what her living situation was fucked up; she was beautiful and in a natural state.

"So what we gonna do about this nigga Bop?" Tez asked knocking me out my daze.

"Do you believe he's the one that been stealing?"

"Hell yeah. I don't steal and we know for damn sure it ain't Echo."

"Then torch em." Echo and Tez both looked at me like I was crazy.

"Man, we don't know for sure it was him." Echo tried to defend him.

"Look my nigga I understand y'all got history with the nigga. I do too but y'all also know how I am about my bread. Nobody fucks with my money period. If you niggas don't like it then y'all gone get handled." I stood to my feet meaning every word. I didn't give a fuck about no history. Shit the nigga should have thought about history before he stole from me. These soft ass niggas know how I move and especially around this time of year. I took my frustrations out on anybody. Since this nigga Bop wanted to play with me like I was some bitch then he'd be my first of what I called Thanksgiving Torch.

"Well, since y'all want the hoe ass nigga alive, I'll just burn his fucking hands off. How about that?" Again, they both looked at each other, and sighed. I shook my head at these niggas especially Echo. Echo knew my get down yet and still he was trying to play captain save a hoe. "Bring the nigga to me, that's it that's all." I walked out of the meeting room and hopped into my whip. I pulled off and headed for the highway. I was gonna head home but for some reason I headed in the direction of the shelter. I needed to see her. Why, I don't know but I needed to see her and now.

When I pulled up, there was some big fat ass security at the door. I parked right in front and hopped out. I walked up to the officer and reluctantly asked him could he call out Cherish. From when I first hopped out my whip the nigga was mugging me. I tried my best to hold my composure because I needed him in order to see Cherish.

"Do you have a last name?" he asked looking at a list.

"Nah."

"Well I can't help you." he said and turned to look away from me.

"I'll just go in, I know how she look."

"I can't let you in here. It's against policy."

"Oh but y'all let me in when I came in this bitch to feed muthafuckas?" I mugged his ass. I was five seconds away from pulling my strap out and putting it in his mouth. But once again I held my composure." I walked away from him shaking my head. I hopped back into my whip and pulled away from the agency. I knew I would see him again and he was gonna wish he had just let me in.

"A cuzzo. Did you get a last name for ol girl?" I asked Shani as soon as she answered hello.

"Who you talkin bout?"

"Cherish."

"Oh no but I can try to get it for you. I gave her my number and I invited her to dinner but she hasn't called."

"Damn aight."

"Let me find out you checking for Cherish?" I could hear her smile through the phone.

"Man, you know me."

"Yes, I do know yo hoe ass." I could tell she rolled her eyes. "Cherish is a really sweet girl. I haven't been knowing her long but we talked for hours and she's sooo cool. If I do this for you yo ass bet not mess over that girl."

"I'm not cousin, I promise."

"And you bet not let Meka attack her or I'mma forget that's yo bitch and beat her ass."

I couldn't help but laugh because I knew she was serious. Shani couldn't stand Meka just as she couldn't stand Poodie her own cousin. But shit Meka and Poodie were like two peas in a pod. They were both heartless and always depended on the next muthafucka to take care of them. They both hated my and Shani's relationship but shit we had been close since kids. Shani was the one that consoled me when my moms was taken. She was also the one that came to visit when I served two years in the county. Shani had my back which is why I did everything for her. I copped her a Spa and I even kept money in her accounts. I helped her buy her first house. And I would die for my cousin. She knew my darkest secrets and was the only one that could snap me back to reality. We were more like sister and brothers instead of cousins but I swear I'll kill for her like she was my child.

"Aight big head girl, I'mma hit you later. Get that info for me too."

"Okay. Love you Bless'cito." she said and laughed. Other than my mother, she's the only one that called me that. I hated it because it reminded me so much of my ma dukes. I hung up the phone and drove out to Mandeville to the Torch. I had a date with this nigga Bop and if he wasn't there when I got there it was gonna be a problem.

When I pulled up to the warehouse I referred to as the torch, I noticed that Taz, Echo and Plot was already here. I hopped out my whip and headed inside because it was time to get this shit going. It's like the minute I walked into this room, my whole vibe changed. Something went through my body that was indescribable. I suffered from some kind of mental state and I knew it was built up anger. Ever since that shit happened to my mom, I couldn't live with myself. I felt like I had failed her. Being a man, I was supposed to protect my mother but I couldn't. I was defenseless and that shit fucked with my mental until this day.

"Please Bless man!" this nigga was already crying and I ain't even do shit.

"Damn, a nigga ain't said or did shit to you and you crying already." I told him as I slid my red gloves on.

"I..I..I know what happens here...come on man. It wasn't me." he cried. I couldn't believe this shit. This was a nigga I had running two of my traps. Right now he was showing signs of weakness.

"So if you know what happens, then why the fuck did you think it was cool to steal some bread from me. Nigga I feed you!" I screamed out to him, spitting in his face.

"I'll pay you back. Come on man. We boys."

"Boys?" I laughed like a deranged psychopath.

"My boys ain't gone steal from me." I told him and pulled his chair close to the pit. The flames had grown covering the entire wall just how I needed it. I yanked him by the arms and held half his arms into the fire burning his hands.

"Ahhhhh!" he let out a gruesome scream.

"If you move Imma toss your entire body inside."

"Ahhhhhh...lord...arhhhh." he cried out as his hands burned. This nigga could scream as loud as he wanted because the walls were sound proof.

29

I watched as Bops' hands burned into crisp forgetting Echo and them were in the room. I'm telling y'all whenever I had to torch someone, I felt like Satan himself. I tuned out everything around and my mind went black. This shit gave me a rush that was better than pussy. Just hearing this nigga scream made me wanna torch his entire body but I was gonna let this nigga survive just to prove a point. When muthafuckas ask why were his hands burned off, he would think about it before he stole from the next muthafucka.

***

When I walked into my crib it was nearly four in the morning. The way I was feeling, I was hoping Meka was asleep because I didn't feel like hearing her nagging. Every time I left the torch, I would feel drained out and not in the mood for the world. That shit always took my energy each time. When I walked into my room and she wasn't lying in the bed I was happy as hell. I knew she was prolly mad I came in at this time so she was more than likely in the guest bedroom. I went into the shower and removed my clothing then climbed in. The minute I hit the water, I had finally begun to relax. I closed my eyes and let the cold water run completely over my waves. I let out a breath of air that seemed like it was trapped inside of me for hours.

As the water covered my body and I was now more relaxed, my mind drifted to Cherish instantly making my dick rise. This girl constantly invaded my mind and I didn't know why. I didn't even know her. I had only two encounters with her and we didn't say much to each other. I needed to have her and just the thoughts alone made me grab my dick. I began to jack it off as I thought about the things I would do to her. I stroked my shit as I envisioned her riding me. Just when I was about to bust...

"Damn you walk up in here at four in the morning and get straight in the shower. I guess you had to wash yo little bitch off you."

I sighed because this bitch had fucked up a good nut. I grabbed my towel and began to lather it ignoring Meka dumb ass. She kept rambling off about nothing important and I continued to ignore her.

"You probably were with that bitch at that shelter. Bum loving ass bitch." she said and tried to walk out the restroom.

I wrapped my hands around her neck and slammed her against the wall.

"Don't you ever in yo life disrespect me again bitch. Do I look like a bitch to you?" I was squeezing her tighter.

"I'm...ahhh." she couldn't talk and I didn't want to hear shit she had to say.

When I let her go she fell to the ground and held her neck. She began coughing dramatically like that shit was gonna make me feel sorry for her. When she stood to her feet, she looked at me with so much hurt in her eyes. Meka wasn't that dark so I could see the red marks I had caused on her neck. I kinda felt bad now but she needed to understand that bitch word wasn't cool.

"What's crazy is, you not mad I called you a bitch. You mad I called that girl a bum. I'm not dumb Blessing. I know you like her. You think I don't remember her from the dealership? Nigga you was on that bitch. Just like at the shelter, you were eyeing that chick like I wasn't there." she said and burst out into tears. I couldn't even say shit because she was right.

I walked over and laid on the bed like nothing ever happened. Meka stood there still crying but what did she expect me to do? I was guilty of everything she just said. Noticing I wasn't about to console her, she shook her head and walked over to the closet. When she grabbed her overnight bag and shoes I knew she was pissed. No matter how much me and this girl argued she would never leave. Shit to be honest she was too scared I would have another chick over. So her leaving me right now, told me I had really hurt her. The question was, did I want to chase after her or let her go? I hated Meka ways, but a nigga grown to love her. She had been around for years and she was close to my family. I'm not gone knock her and say she don't do shit, because she catered to a nigga like a muthafucka. She cooked, she cleaned, did my laundry and she didn't even live here.

Deciding to just let her go, I stayed in the same spot and drifted to sleep with Ms. Cherish on my mind. I don't know why, but I had a feeling things were gonna change in my life once I got her. However, I hoped they changed for the better because I needed it. *Maybe baby girl would be the calm that I needed.* I thought drifting off.

CHAPTER 6

Cherish

"Oh my god. Some guy is in the front for you and he's really freaking hot." Amy one of the staff members, ran over to me and said,
"Huh? Whos..."

"Put your shoes on child and go." she said eagerly, smiling from ear to ear. I lifted from my cot and slid into my sandals. It was nine in the morning and I just got back from taking Miracle to school. I called myself going back to bed but so much for that.

I walked to the entrance of the shelter and nobody was out front. I looked over at Danny but I quickly reconsidered asking him who it was. I turned around to head back inside and suddenly my name was called. I turned around and my heart began to pound. I don't know why but I became nervous as hell.

"Come take a ride with me." Blessing said then looked over at Danny.

"Ride with you? I can't...I have to.."

"I'm not gone bite ma. Just come on." he said and didn't give me a chance to answer. When I looked at Danny, he rolled his eyes like the bitch he was so that made me agree to go along on the ride. Miracle didn't get out of school until 2:30 so I had plenty of time to kill. I walked over to a beautiful red Bentley truck and Blessing was already inside waiting. When I opened the door, I was hit with a loving smell from his cologne and the scent of new car air freshener. I hopped into the plush leather seat nervous as I buckled my seat belt.

"Where are you taking me?"

"Breakfast or something. You hungry?"

Hell yeah, I'm starving shit. I haven't eaten a good meal in weeks. I thought but I wasn't gonna tell him that.

"Sure." I began to fidget in my seat.

"Stop fidgeting ma. You good." he said then pulled off.

"I'm sorry. I'm just confused as to what you want from me?"

"I don't want nothing from you. I just wanna get to know you?"

"Why?" I asked really not meaning to; it just came out like that.

"To be honest, I don't know. It's just something about you."

"Oh." was all I came back with. I lay back in my seat not knowing what else to say. Every now and then I could feel him watching me and that shit had my palms sweating.

Nearly an hour later we pulled up to a restaurant in La-fayette. It was a nice restaurant that had the best breakfast. Paul had brought me here several times and I really loved their omelets. Just being here made me think of Paul so I instantly became depressed. I let out a sigh when Blessing turned off the ignition. He opened his door so I knew I had to get out. When I stepped out, I looked down at my clothing then bit into my bottom lip.

"You good ma." he told me because he knew I was uncomfortable with what I had on.

When we walked inside, I shyly hid behind his back as he told the host we needed a seat for two. She walked us over to a table in the far back with a nice window view. I slid into the booth and Blessing did the same. Instead of picking up his menu he just watched me.

"Umm...I...I..Umm."

"You know you cute when you fidget." he told me and

34

smiled. The way he was watching me was lust mixed with him studying me.

"I'm sorry. I'm just nervous."

"I make you nervous Cherish?" he asked and I nodded my head yes. "Good you should be."

"And why is that?" I asked now interested in what he had to say.

"Because I'm a deadly muthafucka." he spoke as if it was nothing. "But for you, I can be calm." he smiled but he still had this look in his eyes.

I quickly broke his eye contact as I fumbled with the menu. I was a straight nervous wreck and now I wish I hadn't come.

Two hours later, Blessing had finally opened me up. We chit chatted about all types of things. We discussed everything from the restaurant's food to music. When the subject about Thanksgiving came up, he looked off into space. I wanted to ask him what bothered him but I didn't want to seem nosey.

"You ready to roll?" he asked, sliding his plate from in front of him.

"Yeah, if you're ready." I replied and he slid from inside the booth. He dropped a fifty dollar tip on the table like it wasn't nothing. He then grabbed the small of my back and escorted me out the restaurant to his car. He opened my door first so I reached over to open his. When he got in he just looked at me and mumbled.

"Yeah you the one."

"Huh?"

"My pops always told me if a girl opens your car door she's the one."

"Well, it's selfish of me not to. Especially since you opened mines." he nodded his head once and started the car.

"You ready to go back or is it cool if we hang out?"

"Um..sure. I just have to pick my daughter up from school."

"Her little pretty ass. What school she go to?"

"Cambridge Elementary."

"Aight."

"Do you have any kids?"

"Nah. No kids."

"You don't want any or you just don't have none?"

"Don't want any. The shit I do for a living, I can't imagine something happening to me and I leave my kids behind. I'm a dangerous man, Cherish. I live a dangerous ass life. So I just think it will be selfish to bring a child into this world and something happens.

"So what is it that you do if you don't mind me asking?"

"I sell dope. And plenty of it." he said again as if selling drugs wasn't a crime. *Yeah this is gonna definitely be my last time seeing him.* I thought. I wasn't into drug dealers. I mean nothing against them, I just wasn't the type of chick to visit jail houses. "You ever fucked with a Dope Boy?" he asked, making me frown. I thought of the conversation Cherry and I had about the book and I smiled inside.

"No. I mean I have cousins that sell drugs but they always kept it away from me." I told him but he didn't reply back. "I'm not green if that's what you think. I just never wanted to be a part of that world. Again he didn't say anything so I got quiet.

Blessing seemed like a cool guy but I could already see he wasn't for me. Not that I was gonna be his girl or anything but he just wasn't for me. I don't know if I struck a nerve with my last statement or what, but he hasn't said anything else to me. I was now ready to go back to the shelter and not bother with him again.

Thinking we were going to the shelter, I was wrong because we pulled up in front of a park. I looked up into the sky because it looked like it would start raining. Weather in New Orleans was weird like that. It could be sunny and start pouring down out of nowhere. Right now the clouds were dark grey and it looked gloomy for it to have been close to noon. When Blessing climbed out the car, I cursed myself because I was wearing sandals. I was wearing a long sleeve sweater because it was always cold inside the shelter but my feet were out.

"What we doing here?" I asked, thinking he was coming to meet someone.

"I just wanna talk to you. Is that a problem?"

"No." I replied, shaking my head. "So what you wanna talk about?"

"First let's talk about how you ended up in the situation you're in?"

"What do you mean?"

"Like your living situation." he said not wanting to insult me.

"It's a long story I prefer not to talk about. However, it's temporary." he nodded his head. That shit was starting to annoy me. I could tell he wanted to say something every time he did that but he held his tongue. "Look Blessing, you really seem like a nice guy. From the looks of it you have everything you need. I mean, you even have a girlfriend that looks like she's doing good. I can't compete with that. I don't have anything to offer you and if it's pussy you want, I'm sorry but I'm not the sleep around type." I told him then turned to walk away. He pulled me by the hand and pulled me back to him. He made me look at him and his face softened as I stared at his beautiful lips.

"Pussy not an issue with me. I get pussy thrown at me wherever my feet hit the pavement. I'm not out here moved by these bitches. I'd rather jack my dick off and go to sleep. The only thing moves me in this world is money." he said, still making me look at him. "Now, as far as my girlfriend, yeah I got a girl and if I gave a fuck about her I wouldn't be right here trying to get to know you. As far as what you don't have, or your living situation, I don't give a fuck about that shorty. I see a genuine person in you. I'm tired of these hoes out there that don't see shit but dollar signs. From the first day I saw you in the dealership it was something about the way yo eyes sparkled."

The dealership. I thought back to that day. "Come here." he told me and pulled me over to a bench. We took a seat and we began to chat. He asked me questions about Miracle and personal questions about myself like what did I enjoy doing and even what I majored in in college. This man had me blushing like I was in high school all over again. By the time I looked up, it was almost time to get Miracle so I asked him could we leave. He nodded his head and stood to his feet.

"So what now?" I asked him as we walked side by side towards the car.

"That I don't know." he replied then got quiet. The sound of a bell made Blessing and I look over. A horse and carriage was passing by with a huge pumpkin and a flowering embroidered around a sleigh.

"Oh my god that is so beautiful." I beamed as I watched the horse and carriage pass us by. The man riding the horse waved, making me smile as I waved back. "I love the holidays." I turned to Blessing waiting for a response but it was like his demeanor had changed.

"Come on." he said and walked away from me and climbed into the car. He reached over to open my door just in time. Hard rain drops began to pour from the sky hitting the windshield like rocks. He pulled from the park and hopped on the highway. Because he didn't say anything I didn't either. Instead I just laid back in my seat. He had turned the heater on and I got more relaxed. Before I knew it, I had dozed off.

***

"Aye ma." I opened my eyes to Blessing's voice. I lifted from my seat and looked around.

"Go get yo baby." he said, then pulled his phone from his pocket and began texting. I climbed out of the car and headed into Miracle's school. Because it was still raining I quickly ran inside trying hard not to get wet. When I reached her class, the teacher called out her name and she flew out the classroom right into my arms.

"How was school baby?"

"It was good. We had pizza today." she said smiling. Miracle loved pizza so much every time they had pizza for lunch she would brag about it.

I began making small talk with her until we reached Blessing's car. I opened the back door for her and she climbed in.

"Hi Blessing." she said surprising the hell out of me.

"Hi Miracle." he smiled back, shocking me even more. "How was school?" he asked her as he started the car.

"It was good today. We had pizza." she giggled making both us laugh.

"You must love pizza." he told her then focused on the road.

"Yess it's my favorite."

"Miracle you have your seat belt on?" I asked her then looked to the back to make sure she did. After making sure Miracle was secure, I looked over at Blessing who looked deep in thought. I then focused my attention out the window and watched the rain. It seemed like it wasn't letting up anytime soon but I didn't mind. I loved the rain because not only was it soothing, the air was fresh afterwards.

CHAPTER 7

Blessing

Pulling up to Famous pizza, I parked the car and climbed out. When Miracle said she loved pizza a nigga beamed. I loved pizza too and I really liked Famous pizza. Other than just their food, they had an arcade inside, so Miracle could run around and enjoy herself. I assumed living in that bullshit shelter she didn't get out much. Just seeing her eyes light up now had a nigga feeling good inside. I swear this was the prettiest little girl in the world. She looked just like Cherish except she had light brown eyes and jet black curly hair. Cherish was a lighter brown. Other than that they looked identical. Miracle even had Cherish's pretty big smile with her wide mouth ass.

"Blessing, I'm gonna be sick." Cherish reluctantly getting out of the car.

"I'll take care of you." I assured her then motioned for her to get out. When she got out, she grabbed Miracle's hand and they walked ahead of me. Just watching them two made me wonder what life would be like if I had them in my world. After talking to Cherish today, a nigga was really feeling her. The only thing threw me off was the part when she said she loved the holidays. That shit shifted my mood and told me I would have to stay away from her for a minute. Just seeing how she beamed when she saw that bullshit Thanksgiving float going by, I didn't want to spoil it for her. I was no holiday type nigga. During this time of the year, I was a stone cold killer. Not that I wasn't one all year, the holidays only added to my anger.

"Can we get chicken too Blessing?" Miracle asked, bringing me out my daze.

"You can have whatever you want Princess." I told her and scooped her into my arms. She began giggling shyly reminding me so much of her mother. When I first picked Cherish up her ass was nervous as hell. After we began talking she started to relax but her ass was still bashful as hell.

"What you want?" I looked over to Cherish.

"We just ate fatty."

"Man, that was over two hours ago. I'm hungry as fuck."

"Ohh, Blessing said a bad word." Miracle said laughing.

"My bad Princess."

"Just get me a salad." she said just as it was our turn to order. I stepped up to the counter and ordered a large pizza, some hot wings and a salad for Cherish. We then went to the table to wait for them to bring our food. Since the park shit was kinda awkward between us I spent most of my time talking to Miracle. Cherish sat on the sideline just watching us interact. I kinda felt bad because I could see she was slightly sad. A nigga was already fucking up, and this was our first time out together.

After we were done eating, Miracle and I went to play a few games. Meka had texted me three times saying she was hungry but I ignored her. The last text I got from her had me feeling kinda guilty so I told Miracle it was time to leave. When she began to pout, I promised her I'd bring her back tomorrow. She lit up with a huge smile then ran over to the table where Cherish sat.

"Let's roll ma." I told Cherish and she quickly got up from her seat. When Miracle grabbed my hand, that shit blew me back. This girl was getting attached to a nigga, and it was a good and bad feeling. Like I said, I needed to stay away from Cherish for a minute which would mean I had to stay away from Miracle. And I knew this would be fucked up.

Driving back to the shelter, I hated I had to take them back to that place. That wasn't no place for Miracle but shit what else could I do; especially right now. Miracle was a kid so these holidays were important to her. What kid didn't like holidays? As a kid, I loved sitting at my mom's dinner table eating turkey with my family. Shit, on Christmas I would stay up all night just to open my gifts at six am. Now I hate these days. Thanksgiving was right around the corner and after that I had to deal with bullshit ass Christmas.

"Mommy, I don't wanna go in there. Can I go to your house Blessing." Miracle asked sadly.

"Come on, baby. Blessing has to go."

"But I don't wanna go in there." she crossed her arms and began throwing a fit.

"Miracle, I'll be back to take you for pizza okay?" I told her and her facial expression changed.

"You promise?" she asked through a pair of big pretty eyes.

"Pinky swear." I told her and lifted my pinky up for her to shake. She jumped out of the car and ran towards the door of the shelter.

"Thank you." Cherish said looking into the car. I nodded my head at her and she turned to walk away. I watched as she walked towards the door. She looked back at me one last time and our eyes met with each other. She looked so sad the shit made me feel worse. I laid my head back in my seat trying to get my mind right before pulling off. *Was I ready to be a step daddy?* I thought thinking about Miracle. It wasn't even the fact of being a step dad, but was I ready to celebrate these holidays? I knew I was moving fast but just being with them today made me want to wake up to them every day.

Just as fast as I had the thought, I shook it off. Like I told Cherish, I didn't want kids because I lived too dangerous. Meka constantly asked me to give her a baby and I declined her dumb ass all the time. Speaking of the devil, my phone went off again and I knew it was her. Instead of answering, I drove towards the dealership to take her something to eat. Since the day I choked her out she hadn't been back to my crib. We actually didn't talk for a few days until she texted me last night asking did she leave her black boots. I knew that was bullshit, however it worked. That one question turned into a full fledged text session. I ended up texting with her for two hours until I passed out on the sofa.

***

"Ohhh, baby yess!" Meka screamed out as she held the headboard to my king sized bed. I had her in a doggystyle position banging her back out. We had been going at it for over an hour straight and for some reason I couldn't nut. We had changed positions five times and nothing was working.

"I'm cumming daddyyy. Ohh, I'm cumming." she bust all over my dick for the fourth time. Again my dick had gone limp inside of her and I didn't understand why.

"What's wrong?" she stopped bouncing looking back at me.

"Shit, a nigga tired." I lied to her.

"Since when you tired?" she said knowing I had lied.

"Shit, I been running around all day."

"Um hmm." she said and moved from in front of me. She got out the bed and headed into the restroom. When I heard her using the restroom, I laid down on my back and just stared at the ceiling. I fell into a daze as Cherish crossed my mind. This girl had been on my mind since I dropped her off yesterday. I wanted so bad to call just to hear her voice but I remembered she said she didn't have a phone. Another part of me wanted to go up to the shelter but I was trying to keep true to my word and stay away from her.

When I heard the shower come on, I looked towards the restroom, and I could see Meka hopping into the water. I lifted from my bed and pulled my phone from my pants. I dialed Shani's number and waited for her to answer. When she didn't, I hung up and called back. On the second time, she answered, sounding out of breath.

"What you doing and why you ain't answer?"

"Nigga, cause I'm trying to get some dick. And why the fuck you whispering?"

"TMI, my nigga." we both laughed. "But check it, you talk to Cherish?"

"No why?"

"We kicked it yesterday but I don't know man."

"Hold on nigga, damn." she told whoever was in her background.

"Tell that bitch ass nigga hold tight before I come over there and pistol whoop his ass." I told her annoyed.

"I'm not telling him that with yo crazy ass. Anyway, what happened when y'all kicked it?"

"I don't know cuzzo. Shit was cool. We picked her daughter up and took her to Famous."

"So what the fuck happened?" she asked, and I could hear the nigga in the background smack his lips.

"Nigga, you can get the fuck on." the phone got muffled but I could hear her telling the guy. That's another reason I loved Shani. No matter what, I always came first. Here she was in the middle of getting some dick and she had put that shit on hold for me and my problems. "Hello." she said coming back into the phone.

"Like I was saying. Shit was all good, until, some Thanksgiving float went by and she said how she loved the holidays. That shit kinda rubbed me wrong."

"Bless, everybody not going through the shit you going through. Did you tell her about that night?"

"Hell nah, I ain't trying to scare her off."

"Good."

"But look this what really got me. Her daughter man, I felt myself getting attached. You know how I am about kids."

"You know you really need help. You gone miss out on a good girl because of your past. You can't keep doing this to yourself. Give her a chance."

"I want to but shit complicating." I sighed hard. "Can you do me a favor?"

"What nigga?"

"Take her this phone for me tomorrow. At least I could hear her voice."

"Man, I swear you weird as fuck. Aight, bring the phone in the morning foo."

"Aight, good looking. Let me go before this bitch get out the shower."

"You ain't shit Blessing."

"Duhh." we laughed and hung up. Right on cue, I heard the shower water stop running so I put my phone back into my pocket. I laid back down, and again I got lost in my thoughts of Cherish. I was happy as hell I would be able to hear her voice. It's like tomorrow couldn't come fast enough. I knew this was some weird shit but I needed to hear her voice.

CHAPTER 8

Cherish

C limbing from my cot sluggishly, I went towards the front door because I was being paged to the front. When I walked to the front area, Shani was standing there smiling from ear to ear. A part of me wished it was Blessing, but of course not, because just like I thought he was done with me. After the day he dropped me off, I hadn't heard from him. It really didn't surprise me because the way he was acting when he dropped me off I knew I wouldn't see him again. The entire time him and Miracle were in the pizza parlor, he didn't bother with me once. Instead, he left me sitting at the table while him and Miracle ran around playing games. That entire night I wrecked my brain wondering what it could be but I had given up. Blessing was hella mysterious and he held back a lot of his personal life. It was crazy because he didn't have a problem telling me he kills people and sells drugs but the nigga wouldn't tell me what the fuck bothered him so much about Thanksgiving. I didn't care about his lifestyle. I wanted to know him as a person. I wanted to know about his childhood and even things he enjoyed doing. Just in one day he knew my whole life and all I knew about him was, his name and his age; oh and he's a bad guy and dope boy. I rolled my eyes at my own thoughts.

"Hey stranger." Shani said, reaching out for a hug.
"Don't get too close ma." I told her and began coughing.
"Ohh, you look a hot mess."

"I know." I replied sounding like I was holding my nose. I was stuffed up and I had a slight fever. "Thanks to your cousin, my ass caught a cold."

"That's actually what I'm here for. He wanted me to give you this." she said and handed me a box. I studied the box and it was a brand new iPhone X. As bad as I wanted the phone I didn't want shit from him.

"Tell him no thank you." I said and handed her the phone back.

"He's gonna die if I don't give you this and you don't know my cousin. That man is crazy." she laughed but she was right. That nigga was crazy literally. I figured that out when he bragged about being dangerous as if you could apply for a position as a killer.

"I'm cool Shani. I don't want anything from him."

She put the phone back into the bag she was carrying and we both stood there quiet.

"Is it something about Thanksgiving he hates because the day you guys were here he looked like he didn't want to be bothered. At first, I thought it was the shelter until we went out yesterday. It was as if anything that had to do with Thanksgiving bothered him. Hell, I got dumped before I made the list all because I mentioned Thanksgiving."

"Ummm...he's just not in the best spirits around the holidays." she said, and I could tell she was hiding something. I don't know if he had a troubled past but I wasn't one to judge. Look at my situation shit. I wished they both would just understand it.

"So how long are you here for?" she asked me looking around.

"January."

"Oh that's not bad.

"I'm gonna go back to lay down. It feels like I'mma pass out any minute. I told her feeling dizzy. Thanks to Blessing I was sick as hell and didn't have any medicine. I had even got Miracle sick so she missed school today and she was gonna miss tomorrow.

"Okay ma, you feel better." she smiled and headed for the

door.

"Shani," I called her name and she spent around to look at me.

"Thank you." I told her and smiled weakly.

"You're welcome. And just because you don't wanna be bothered with him you can call me." she said, making me smile hard. I nodded my head and mouth okay. She walked out the door, and I headed back to my cot to get some rest. I was gonna curl up with my baby under the cover and try my best to sweat this cold out.

***

"Cherish. Cherish." I opened my eyes and Cherry was standing over me. I was feeling worse than I did when I went to sleep so I really didn't wanna be bothered.

"You have a phone call. They called your name over the intercom three times. Yo ass been knocked out."

"Who is it?" I asked, not wanting to move. I sat up and it felt like my entire body was in pain. I knew it couldn't have been anyone but Blessing or Shani because no one called me or came to visit.

I walked over to the phone and quickly picked it up.

"Hello?" I said unbothered, waiting to hear Blessing's voice.

"Yes, Ms. Hamilton."

"Yes, who's this?"

"Hi, it's Ms. Gillet from the District Attorney office.

"Okay." I said, wondering why she was calling me.

"I wanted to inform you that Mr. Paul Jones will be coming up for release soon." Just hearing Paul's name froze me in my tracks. I fell into a deep daze until I heard her calling my name.

"Ms. Hamilton, are you there?"

"I'm sorry...yes...yes...I'm here. When is his release date?"

"He's being released December 3rd. I wanted to inform you about this information for your safety. If by any chance he con-

48

tacts you or comes anywhere near you please call the local police if you in danger. Also give me a call because I'll make sure to have him locked back up in no time."

"Okay. I really appreciate the call." I told her and disconnected the line. I was glad she had called to give me a heads up but I was the least bit worried. I knew Paul couldn't get to me here and once I moved he really wouldn't find me. My information was unlisted due to protection.

When I walked back over to my cot, Cherry was laying on it with Miracle. I thanked her and she stood to her feet to leave. As she turned around, she bumped into Camille nearly knocking her down.

"Watch where the fuck you going." Camille told her then looked at me with a mug.

"Watch where the fuck you going hoe." Cherry told her frowned up.

"Keep talking and I'll write yo homeless ass up." Camille threatened.

"At least I'm homeless and happy. You got a roof over your head and you still miserable with yo dickless ass. What, you mad Blessing checking for my girl and not you? Well, keep being mad because that's her new boyfriend."

"Cherry." I called out to her. I didn't need Camille in my business with her hating ass. Instead of Camille saying anything else she stormed off upset.

"Man, I'm tired of that hoe. Bitch always talking about she gone write somebody up. She ain't gonna write up shit. If I get kicked out, I'm telling on her hoe ass too. I got her and Morgan on my cell phone making out."

I couldn't do shit but burst out laughing. Cherry was crazy as hell and I couldn't blame her. Camille stayed fucking with us for no reason. Well, at first it was for nothing. Now she really hated me over a man I didn't even have.

"So who was that on the phone, yo boo?" Cherry asked, shifting the subject from Camille. Because she was the only one that knew my story. I began to explain what the call was about. Right now, I wish it had been Blessing instead. We began talking and got lost into our conversation like we did every time we talked about Paul. I had basically told Cherry my whole life story so she was familiar with all of this. We talked about this for hours of the night. As much as I tried to act like it didn't bother me, I was a bit paranoid. Paul was dangerous, and because of Miracle, I knew he was gonna eventually find me. I knew the type of guy he was so he would for sure involve the courts. However, he wouldn't be granted custody because by the time everything took place I'd be moved into my own place.

CHAPTER 9

Blessing

"Can you please be on time." Meka said as she hopped out my whip.

"That's why you should have drove yo own shit. You know I got business to handle."

"Everything is always more important than me." she said smacking her lips. I grabbed the bridge of my nose to refrain from cursing her ass out. She had three whips, and I had plenty cars she could have drove. I knew her ass was only doing this to keep track of what I had going but little did she know, her ass would be catching Uber fucking with me.

"Bye Meka." I told her and she stormed off towards the dealership. I couldn't wait for her to get out because I wanted to call Cherish just to hear her voice.

I pulled out my phone and dialed the number to the iPhone I had copped her but the shit went straight to voicemail. I called a second time and got the same result so I dialed Shani's number to make sure she had given Cherish the phone.

"Hello."

"Cuzo, what's up?"

"Shit, at the Spa working. Where you been? I been calling you since yesterday?"

"Shit, just handling business. Did you handle that for me?"

"I went up there but she wouldn't take the phone."

"Fuck you mean she wouldn't take the phone?"

51

"Nigga, she wouldn't take it. She said she don't want anything from you. And she also mentioned the day y'all went out. She started asking me questions about you."

"Like what?"

"Thanksgiving." was all she said, and I knew exactly what that meant.

"What you tell her?"

"I told her to talk to you about it. I wasn't gonna tell her nothing. When you ready to have that talk with her you tell her. But yeah, she pissed at you. And she's sick as hell, thanks to you having that poor girl out in the rain."

"Damn. Aight."

"Maybe you should try to take it to her."

"Okay. Imma swing by and grab it."

"Nah nigga, I'm keeping this." she said and laughed. She knew I wasn't gonna tell her no so I was gonna have to take a trip to T Mobile.

"Spoiled ass."

"So what nigga, bye." she said and hung up. I pulled off from Meka's job and headed to get Cherish another phone. Because Shani mentioned her being sick, I was also gonna head to Walgreens and grab her some meds. Cherish not accepting the phone let me know she was upset with a nigga so I had to make shit right with her.

After leaving the phone store, I drove to the Walgreens that was around the corner from the shelter. I headed inside and went to the medicine aisle. I picked up some Nyquil, Dayquil, a pack of halls, some tea and a few cans of soup. I even grabbed some children's medicine just in case Miracle got sick too. Making my way to the register, I piled everything on the counter then went into my pocket to pay.

"Hey Blessing." I turned around and Camille was standing there holding a blue basket filled with all types of shit.

"Sup." I nodded my head to her. My eyes moved down to her blouse that was exposing her big ass titties. Them muthafuckas had to be some double d's. She was also wearing a skirt that didn't even make it to her knees. It hugged her curves and I could see her fat ass from the front.

"What you doing on this side of town?" she asked, trying to make conversation.

"Same thang you doing on this side of town." I replied smartly.

"Well, I'm going to work."

"Dressed like that?" I shook my head then turned to the cashier.

"Forty-two ninety-seven." the cashier said, placing the stuff into a bag. I handed her the money then made my way for the door.

"Make sure you call me. Let's hang out." Camille said just as I was walking out.

"Aight." I told her then left. I was definitely gonna call her. I was gonna do more than call her. I was gonna fuck baby girl brains out then put her thirsty ass on my block list.

When I pulled up to the shelter, I jumped out and headed to the door. I gave the security Cherish first and last name, and I was granted entrance. It was the same security from last time and again the nigga was mugging me. I don't know if he knew me from the streets or him and Cherish had something going on because this nigga was bugged out by my presence.

When I walked in, the front counter paged Cherish and told me to have a seat. I went and sat down at an empty table and waited for her to come out. Looking around the shelter, I took in how nice it actually looked. Minus the bullshit Thanksgiving decorations the place was pretty clean and it actually didn't smell too bad.

"What are you doing here?" I looked up to Cherish who wore a scowl on her face like she wasn't too pleased with me.

"I came to bring you some medicine. How you feeling?"

"I'm fine Blessing."

"You don't look it." I told her because she looked sick as hell. Her nose was red, her eyes were red and she looked weak.

"I don't need anything from you." she said ready to turn around.

"Look ma, I don't normally do shit like this so the fact that I'm trying, you could at least give me credit for that. I apologize about getting you sick and whatever else you mad about we can talk about it." she stopped and looked at me. I could tell she wanted to talk shit but instead she took a seat. As soon as she sat down, Camille walked through the door and mugged Cherish. Cherish's facial expression matched Camille's and I could see already this Camille chick was gonna be a problem. Cherish focused her attention back to me, and I could see she was more annoyed with what just happened.

"First of all, you're a liar. You had my daughter asking for you all day because of a stupid promise you made to her. Then, the day I was with you, you just changed up on me. You fed me all that bullshit to make me feel better for what? To just disappear for five days?" she spat. Just looking her in the eyes, I could tell she was hurt. It was crazy because it was written all over her face. This chick was really digging a nigga.

"I be busy ma. You just don't know how complicated my life is."

"So why come in and complicate mines?" she replied sadly. Just looking at this girl, sick and all, her eyes told it all. It's like they pleaded for me and the shit was making me weak. I wasn't no weak nigga but this damn girl was showing me I actually had a soft spot. The only woman in my life I was submissive to was Shani. I wasn't even this submissive to my step mother.

"I don't wanna complicate things in your life. I wanna be the one to make you happy."

"Well, you have a crazy way of showing it." she rolled her eyes.

"Well, let me have another chance to show you."

"I can't Blessing. You have a girl and I know your kind. All you're gonna do is make me fall in love with you just to

54

friendzone me. I mean, what else can you do with me?" *Damn.* I thought because she was right. Anytime this girl was in my presence I'd forget about Meka. Not to mention, I was a dawg ass nigga. But I liked Cherish so I know I wouldn't dog her out like the rest of these bitches.

"I want you to be more than a friend. I'mma make you my bitch one day. I just gotta figure out how."

"Your bitch?" she asked with her nose turned up.

"Man, you know what I mean. Here." I told her and handed her the phone. She looked at the box but she didn't say a word. "I need to hear yo voice every day. I'mma figure this shit out with Meka, but like I said, I want you to be more than a friend. Just give me some time alright?" the look in her eyes told me I had her but I needed to hear her say it.

"What do you want from me?" she asked sincerely.

"To be my peace." I jested but was honest. She just looked at me and she didn't understand what I meant. It was too much to explain but she would soon find out. I needed this girl in my world because it seemed like she was the only one that could bring me peace. The way I was moving in these streets, nothing or no one made me feel as peaceful as Cherish. Not only the way she looked at me, but her aura whenever she was around. I didn't have to be this tough ass nigga in the streets when I was with her.

"I'm Cherish." she extended her hand and smiled. At first, I was puzzled but then I caught on.

"I'm Daddy but people call me Bless." I grinned and we both laughed. It felt damn good to see her smile. Now I only had one problem; I had to make it up to Miracle.

CHAPTER 10

Cherish

L ooking through my bags of clothing I was so caught up on what the hell I was gonna wear. I had promised Shani I would finally come over for dinner. Blessing didn't know I was coming, and I hoped like hell he wouldn't be there. Shani had explained to me that he lived in his own house and that his girlfriend also had her own home. Just knowing Blessing didn't have a girlfriend at home made me feel better about the situation. However, I would only be his friend until he figured things out. I didn't understand how he talked so much crap about the girl but he was still with her. If he loved her then he loved her. That was his problem. But if he thought he was gonna be with us both, he had the right idea just the wrong person. I wasn't no homewrecker type of chick, so I wasn't trying to step on her toes. But the fact still remained, this man came for me. No matter how much I tried to push him away he would come for me.

Ever since the day he left, which was three days ago, we had talked all day and all night on the phone. I was still trying to get the hang of using the phone because it was the newest iPhone that had come out. This crazy boy had stored himself in the phone as *My Future* and that only added to my crush. Knowing he was a busy man, it made me feel good because he would call just to say he was thinking about me. He would even send me texts with kissy faces that would make my day. Whenever I didn't answer my phone, his crazy ass would talk mess. I couldn't even use the bathroom without having the phone glued to my side. I had finally let him talk to Miracle and just like I knew she brought up the promise he had made. He promised to take her out this weekend, and I swear if he lied to my baby again I wasn't messing with his ass.

Be my peace. Replayed over and over in my mind constantly. I didn't really know what he meant by that but just hearing him say it was gratifying.

Once I had finally found an outfit, I headed for the showers. Miracle was already dressed so Cherry had her on her cot playing around on her tablet. I quickly went into the shower and soaped up as fast as I could. I had about thirty minutes before Shani said she would arrive so I had to make it quick. Once I was done, I slid into a pair of acid washed skinny jeans and a pair of ankle boots with a three-inch heel. I chose to wear my Tulane University sweater that hung off the shoulder because once again it was raining. Because of my look, I brushed my hair into a sleek bun at the top and made sure it was nice and big. Of course, I had to brush my baby hairs because they were natural and would eventually come out my bun. By the time I was done, I heard my name being paged so I headed over to grab Miracle.

"Have fun. And bring me a plate back." Cherry laughed.

"Okay." I smiled to her then headed off.

"Bye, Cherry." Miracle waved at her excitedly. My baby was happy to be leaving this place because the only place she ever went was school. Today they had a free day which was perfect timing for the dinner. Thanks to Blessing we were both feeling much better. Miracle and I walked hand in hand towards the front and I couldn't wait to see Shani. Over the course of the days, if I wasn't on the phone with Blessing I was talking to her. We had become pretty close and she was the coolest ever. Well next to Cherry.

***

When we pulled up to The Love's residence I was appalled at how beautiful their home was. It was in a nice part of town that looked really expensive. When Shani opened her car door I opened mines and stepped out. I pulled Miracle from the back seat and waited for Shani to lead the way. When we walked inside the home, it was even more beautiful on the inside. It was extremely large and nicely decorated. I followed Shani down a long hallway that lead into a kitchen. When we walked in, an older lady was standing at the stove stirring a huge pot.

"Hey aunty." Shani chimed walking over to hug her.

"Hey baby." she turned around and her eyes fell from me to Miracle. A wide smile spread across her face as she kneeled down to greet her.

"How are you doing pretty lady?"

"Good." Miracle blushed.

"Aunty, this is Cherish, Blessing's real wife." aunty raised one eyebrow and smirked looking me over.

"I'm not." I snickered making them both laugh out.

"Well, I'm glad you two could join us. There's pink panties in the fridge, dinner will be ready soon.

"You and your pink panties. Get some Henny up in here." Shani teased.

"Some who?" aunty said and dropped her hands down to her wide hips. I couldn't do anything but laugh. I knew I was gonna like aunty because she was so heart feeling. Just being in her presence, I could tell she was a genuine lady.

"You want some Pink Panties?" Shani turned from the fridge.

"Um...I have my baby."

"Girl, she's fine and yo ass ain't driving." she pulled the mug from the fridge and walked over to the counter. She grabbed two glasses from the cabinet above and began filling them up.

"Can I help you cook?" Miracle asked showing all of her

fronts.

"Girl, you can't cook." Shani told her and they both laughed. On the way here, Shani talked to Miracle more than she talked to me. I knew it was because Miracle's ass asked a million questions so I didn't mind.

"Sure you can help me." Aunty told her and pulled her to the sink to wash her hands.

"We going outside." Shani pulled me from inside the kitchen and out the side door that led to the kitchen.

When we made it outside, there was a patio set we took a seat on. We instantly began to chat. After a few drinks, I was good and buzzed and Shani kept feeding me the liquor. I was feeling so good, I didn't even know where we were gonna sleep tonight and right now I didn't care. I knew we were gonna be out past 8pm and I also knew Danny wasn't gonna let me in. Ever since he saw me with Blessing, he had been acting worse. I tried my best to keep my distance from him just like Camille because I wasn't gonna be there forever.

"Uh oh." Shani said and looked towards the driveway. A car had just pulled in but the only thing I could see was headlights. Suddenly, out stepped Blessing but I don't think he had seen me yet. Next, his girlfriend stepped out the car and slammed the door shut behind her. *I knew this would be a bad idea.* I thought watching as Blessing entered the gate. When he neared us, he frowned up surprised. I smiled short and turned to take a sip of my drink.

"Sup Shani? How you doing Cherish?" he acknowledged.

"Hey." I spoke nervously and tried to look away. I was hoping I wasn't imposing on him because I didn't wanna start anything between him and his girl.

"What y'all got up?" he asked looking from Shani to me.

"I am hungry." his girlfriend snarled.

"Okay, what's stopping you from eating. Bye." Shani shot with an evil glare. When Blessing chuckled under his breath, I knew right then these two were pretty close. Upon talking to

Shani, I could tell she didn't like Meka.

"Blessing!!!" we all looked over and Miracle was running full speed towards him. She ran up on him and wrapped her arms around his legs. Meka smacked her lips and stormed into the house fuming.

"What's up little ma? How you doing?"

"Good." she chuckled. It's like this was all she knew how to say whenever someone asked how she was. "I was helping Glama cook."

Oh boy. This girl been here two hours and already claiming people.

"Who?" Blessing asked her confused.

"Glamaaa." she emphasized.

"Why you didn't tell me you were coming?" he put Miracle down and looked over at me.

"Why, is there a problem? Because I can leave. I don't wanna cause any..."

"Girl please. You my fucking company." Shani ranted before Blessing could answer.

"Nah, it's not a problem. Shit, had I known you were here, I would have came solo." he looked into the house.

"Dinner ready." Aunty stuck her head out the door to inform us.

"Good, because a nigga starving." Blessing said and walked into the house. This shit was gonna be awkward as hell. A part of me wanted to just leave. Then again I knew Shani wasn't having it.

When we walked in, the table was set and Meka sat there with her nose turned up. Mr. Love, who I had met about an hour ago, sat at the head of the table. I took a seat across from Blessing, but on the other side which put me in front of Meka. She had picked up her phone and then sat it back down on the table. Moments later, another chick had emerged from upstairs and sat next to Meka. As soon as she sat down, they started whispering amongst each other. I knew they had to be discussing me because every now and then they both would look up. "Ding." my phone chimed so I pulled it from my hand bag.

My Future: *You look pretty asf*

I looked up and my eyes met Blessing's. He had his phone in his hand and didn't give two fucks his girl was sitting on the side of him. I slid the button on the side of my phone so it would mute the sound. I then responded to his text trying hard not to smile.

Me: *thank you and you're crazy*

My Future: *crazy for you. Can you stay with me tonight?*

Me: *I don't know, Bless. I have Miracle*

My Future: *So. you act like I'm trying to fuck you. Girl you ain't ready for this dick yet.*

Me: *nah I'm not lol*

Shani: *y'all both crazy*

I looked over and Shani who was grinning from ear to ear. I was glad they both had texted me because I was trying hard to ignore these two childish ass females that sat at this table.

"So you just gonna disrespect me like I'm not sitting here?" Meka jumped up from her seat. Blessing looked up at her unmoved.

"Sit the fuck down before I forget my parents right here." He told her without even looking her way.

"Girl, you let him talk to you any kind of way." the other girl chimed in.

"Mind yo fucking business." Blessing spat.

"Y'all don't start that shit today. Don't y'all see we have company." Mr. Love barked looking around the table.

"She ain't no damn company." the other girl said rolling her eyes.

"She my company bitch now what." Shani jumped to her feet. Things were getting crazy, and I felt like I was the cause. I don't know if they did this all the time but the guilt was taking over me and I was ready to go.

"Umm, I think I'mma just go." I said and went to stand up.

"You ain't going nowhere so sit the fuck down." Blessing spoke calmly, but I could tell he meant it.

"Why the fuck you worried about her leaving or not?" Once again Meka jumped to her feet. "Are you fucking her?" she looked from me to Blessing.

"Man, you sound dumb as fuck. I don't even know this girl."

"You don't know her? You don't know her? It's crazy you don't know her but her fucking daughter just ran to you like y'all were best buddies. I swear you got me fucked up Blessing." she stormed off slamming the door behind her.

"Where the bitch gone go? I drove." he said not so much as cracking a smile. He was in his plate and unmoved by everything that just went on.

"Blessing, watch your mouth." his father told him and he seemed not bothered by his words either. Just looking around the room, I could tell Blessing was spoiled, got his way, and didn't answer to no one. He was also stubborn as hell and I peeped that weeks ago. This boy didn't have any damn filter not even in front of his parents. I know this shit sounds crazy but he turned me on even more. This guy was powerful. The way he ran shit just around me and his family and even the shelter, I could only imagine how he was in the streets. Call me a hoe, I don't care, but I was ready to drop my panties for him right here at this table.

CHAPTER 11

Blessing

"So what you do nigga?"

"Shit, I picked her up and played with her."

"Step Daddyyyy." Echo laughed into the phone. I had called this nigga to hit up the strip club and the conversation went left.

"Fuck you nigga."

"So what you gonna do with her man? Seems like you really digging this chick."

"Shit, honestly, a nigga don't know. I like her like a muthafucka but you know me Echo.

"Well nigga, it sound like yo mind made up. Especially after the way you dog Meka. Man, I gotta meet this chick." he said laughing on the phone.

"Shit, you have." I told him but that's all I was gonna tell him. Well, at least for now. I wasn't embarrassed by Cherish situation. I just was a private type nigga. Echo my boy like a muthafucka and that was just that. We kicked it, he had my back and he also worked for me but in this game their wasn't no friends. Most of the time. I pretty much kept to myself. I couldn't just sit around niggas all day. The only time I did, was in my traps, or in the club.

"Hold on." I told him clicking over.

"Yeah."

"Blessing. oh my God. This bitch ass nigga up here at this

shelter just called me and Cherish all kinds of bitches. They won't let her in so I'mma just take her to my house."

"What?!" I jumped to my feet. "Who is this nigga?"

"This fat ass security nigga at the door of the shelter."

"Aight." I told her as I nodded my head. I had something for this nigga.

Ignoring the fact I had Echo on hold, I headed into my room and grabbed my strap. Meka was laying in my bed still with an attitude watching me. She didn't say one word, and I didn't say it either but the look she gave me let me know she knew something was bothering me. I stormed out my crib and hopped into my BMW. I made my way to Shani's crib. I was gonna make sure Cherish and Miracle were straight before I made my move on this fuck nigga.

When I pulled up to Shani's, her car was in the driveway so I made my way to the door. I used my key and let myself in then stormed through the house to find Cherish. When I found her, she was in the restroom putting Miracle in the tub.

"Come here real quick." I told her then went into the hall to wait. When she walked out, she was fidgeting like always.

"Hey." she said trying not to look at me. I walked up on her and grabbed her chin to make her look at me.

"You straight?" she nodded her head yes. "So you staying here tonight?"

"Yeah I guess."

"So what's up with this nigga? You ever fucked him?" I read her eyes to see if she was gonna lie.

"What? Hell no." I nodded my head and told her I'll be back. I walked away from her and out the door and she watched me all the way until I disappeared. I hopped back in my whip and drove towards the shelter. I was doing a hunnit trying to get there because my adrenaline was pumping. I was sick of this nigga already so hearing he called, not only Cherish, but Shani a bitch, I was gonna have to teach this nigga a lesson.

***

"Ahhhhhh! Please man." this nigga screamed out like a hoe. It was crazy how these niggas was so tough in the streets but once I got a hold of them it was *please man.*

"See, we wouldn't even be going through this if yo fat, fake cop wanna be tough ass understood who I was. Since the first day you saw me up there you had a problem with me. What, you in love with my bitch?" I snatched his head and put his face into the fire.

"Arghhhhhhh!"

"You in love with my bitch nigga?" I raged.

"No...noo...I don't want her. Please." he begged with his face halfway burnt off. I had this nigga in here torching him for over an hour. He was bloody as hell and crying for his dear life. I wanted so bad to just let him go so every time he looked at his face he'd think of me but fuck that. This nigga had to go. I kicked him and the entire chair into the pit and watched this nigga body burn.

"Ahhhhh!" he screamed for about ten seconds until his screams went muffled. I watched his body burn through a pair of black eyes. I watched the flames excitedly as he turned to crisp. Like always I was in a trance and it seemed like every time I torched someone it was more and more fascinating.

***

By the time I walked into Shani's crib it was four in the morning. I wanted to go lay with Cherish but I couldn't be around her like this. Every time I torched someone I went into a zone thinking bout my moms. When I got like this, anything would make me snap. However, I walked into the room where she was sleeping and stood at the door. I watched her as she slept and it's like I fell into another daze. I hadn't known this girl an entire month and already she was getting to me. I had literally just killed a nigga because he called her a bitch.

Just watching Cherish right now gave me the peace I needed so I stood in one spot for a long time. Miracle was inside the other guest room so that told me she expected for me to come back and sleep with her. *Fuck it,* I thought climbing in the bed next to her. I wrapped my arm around her and slid her into my body as close as she could get.

"Ummm." she said stirring in her sleep. "Bless." she purred my name softly.

"Go to sleep Cherish." I told her because like I said I didn't want her to see me like this. I wrapped my hand into hers and didn't say a word. I let her doze back off as I got lost in my thoughts.

"One day you're gonna meet a girl that's gonna make you fall in love. And when you do you gonna be so gone boy yo ass just might hurt something over her."

"I don't want no girlfriend ma. I don't even trust women."

"That's what you say now until you meet somebody that's gonna win you over and have you open like a poet."

"Like daddy got you." we both laughed.

"Yeah son, like yo daddy got me." she stopped washing the dishes and beamed looking out the window above the sink. Just looking in her eyes, I could tell she was in love and that was a look I never wanted to have.

I could vividly hear my mother say those words and I never thought the day would come. Meka was the closest I got to a relationship and I wasn't even in love with her. Cherish was giving me a feeling I'd never felt before. She had my insides cringing every time I saw her ass. When I wasn't with her I thought of her. I was texting cute shit I never texted, and I even stayed on the phone with her all night. Most nights I would leave Meka at home just to talk to Cherish all night. Now I see how moms felt about my dad and no lie the feeling of love hurt. It's like I didn't want nobody around her. I didn't want anyone to have her. Every time she mentioned she would be moving soon I got these crazy feelings in my stomach.

I have never in my life disrespected Meka like this and I really didn't even care. I sat right next to her as I texted Cherish knowing she could look over into my phone. And guess what? I didn't even give a fuck. I loved Meka, but I wasn't in love with her. Even from the first time I met her, up until the first time we fucked, she never gave me the feelings Cherish gives me. She never made me wanna wife her. But with Cherish, I've had visions of her in my crib and raising my kids. I sat right here right now sniffing this girl hair like a manic obsessed and I ain't never did know shit like this. I didn't even cuddle. I had a whole ass bitch at my crib who was prolly crying her eyes out and not even that mattered. I knew it was only a matter of time I was gonna have to cut Meka off. I just didn't want to flat out hurt her but I knew if I didn't do it now, shit would only get worse.

CHAPTER 12

Cherish

I opened my eyes and had to take in where I was. Looking around the room I remembered I was asleep in Shani's guest bedroom. When I tried to lift up, a strong masculine arm held onto me for dear life. And that's when I realized Blessing had climbed into the bed with me last night.

"Blessing, I have to get up." I shook him lightly.

"Lay down ma. Yo ass ain't got no job so you ain't got shit to do." he mumbled without opening his eyes.

"I have to take my baby to school Mr. Know it all."

"I took her already." he said and again he hadn't opened his eyes.

"Oh." I laid back down and snuggled my body into his. I turned to my side and I was face to face with him.

"Stop watching me like a creep and say what's on your mind." he said smirking. I had so much to say that I didn't know what to say first. I really didn't want to speak what was on my mind because I didn't know where I stood with him. After last night at his parents' house, he pretty much dissed his girlfriend for me so that told me he was really interested in me. But now what?

"I just wanna know where I stand with you. Last night was very confusing. I don't wanna seem like I'm moving fast but are we going somewhere with this? I really like you so let me know something."

"Well, for starters, you belong to me now. Let's get that understood now. Oh, and as far as that shelter, you ain't going back there."

"So where am I gonna go?"

"Shit, I don't know. You can go to a hotel or you can stay here."

"No, I don't wanna impose on Shani." I replied thinking about the last time I lived with a woman. Shani was cool as hell but so was Verlin. That's how it always started off until we started bumping heads. "A hotel will cost too much."

"I don't care how much it cost ma; you ain't going back to that shelter." I nodded my head in agreeance because I could tell he meant it. "And last night, I did what I did to show you I don't give a fuck. Meka don't scare me nor control me."

"I hope you never do me like that." I frowned. They say the way you get em, you lose em so I knew it was possible he would do me the same way.

"I'll never do you like that. See, the difference with y'all, I want you. I asked for this. I came looking for you. Meka, on the other hand, forced a relationship out of me. You know why she let me get away with so much? Because I told her from the beginning I wasn't shit. Every time she caught me cheating I told her to leave but she decided to stay behind and deal with my bullshit. So again, I'll never do you like that." Everything he said sounded so good I just hoped his ass meant it. " Let's go to sleep for a minute." he said and scooted my body closer to his. The minute our bodies touched, I could feel his erection through his pants. It had been so long since I been touched, so I bravely rubbed my hand across it to fantasize about it.

"You ain't ready for that." he said and moved my hand. I was so embarrassed I turned to my other side so I wouldn't face him. He snuggled his face into my neck and within seconds he was snoring lightly. I closed my eyes hopping I'd get some sleep but I knew that would be hard to do. My pussy was dripping wet and being in Blessing's arms for the first time had me on cloud nine. This man had full control over, not only my mind, but my body as well. In so little time I submissively fell in love with him and the feeling was insanely crazy. *This nigga done practically came in and rocked my world and I haven't even gotten the dick.* I shook my head at my own thoughts and closed my eyes. I was gonna try hard to go to sleep until it was time to pick up Miracle.

***

Blessing and I pulled up to the shelter after picking up Miracle so we can get our things. Although I couldn't wait to leave this place, I knew I was gonna miss it. Some of the staff was pretty cool and I had pretty much got used to the place. Blessing was gonna pay Amy to sign me off daily so it could look like I was still here and I wouldn't lose my place in line for my apartment. I hopped out the car and headed inside. Blessing was holding Miracle so they stayed in the front. I walked over to my clothing and began tossing them in bags. Once I was done, I did the same with my hygiene and all of Miracle's belongings then headed over to find Cherry.

"What's all that?" she asked looking over the bags I was dragging.

"I'm leaving?"

She eyed me suspiciously.

"Leaving like leaving leaving?"

"Yes. I'm leaving. But I'll still come visit you. You have my number."

"I sure do. But let me guess, you and baby boy are official so I'm assuming that's where you going." she smirked.

"Yes and no. I'm gonna stay in a hotel until my name comes up. Last night, I got into a fight with Danny so Blessing doesn't want me here."

"That bitch ass nigga. Yeah he ain't even show up for work today. They had to call Scott to cover for him. No call no show."

"Yeah, well I hope his ass is somewhere in hell." I hated Danny with a passion. Last night was the last straw and I didn't care about getting kicked out. When Shani brought me here

I knew he wasn't gonna let me in but I still wanted to grab some of my belongings. He denied me entrance like always and jumped ship on Shani. When I heard him yell bitch in her face, I lost it. We argued with that man for nearly an hour until we finally left. I knew Shani was gonna call Blessing, and I was a bit scared because I could tell he was short fused. It was something about the look in his eyes when he came over last night that had me shook. Hours later, he crept into the bed and again something about his voice told me not to challenge what he had said.

"Well call me. I'll come by and see you. As soon as I get my check we'll come up there and chill."

"Okay." I smiled wanting to invite her now. But I knew Cherry all too well. She was the type of chick that wouldn't leave the house broke. When she didn't have any money, she would sit in this shelter until she came up on her next dollar. I couldn't say I didn't blame her because I hated being broke period. Shit, I had a daughter I had to look out for.

I hugged Cherry and made my way to find Amy. As soon as I found her, I hit her with the proposition and with the amount Blessing was offering, I knew she would bite. I also left her my number and told her to call me if need be. After she agreed, I made my way out the door. I handed Blessing the bags I was able to carry and went back for the rest of the stuff. Making three trips I was done so I headed back to him. Blessing grabbed my hand and led me towards the door. He had Miracle on his other side holding her hand as well.

"Blessing." we both turned around to Camille. She stood there with a mug on her face but she wouldn't look at me. "Why you ain't call me?" she asked then finally smirked at me. I slid my hand from in his and looked at him to see what his response would be.

"When you see me with my bitch don't say shit to me yo." he said then grabbed my hand to turn back around. I didn't care for the bitch word but because he checked that bitch, I let it go. I looked back as we were walking out and smiled to her with a wave. She had a scowl on her face that told me she was pissed.

But that was her bad for trying to taunt me.

As we headed for Blessing's car, I heard my name being called so I turned in the direction and it was Bernard. I smiled because I hadn't seen him in almost six months.

"Hey Bernard."

"Hey Cherish. Hey Miracle," he said giving Miracle a high five."

"Hii Bernard." Miracle smiled. She loved Bernard because he had been around for years. He was the cop on the case with Paul and since, he has been really nice to us.

From the sideline, I could feel Blessing mugging me.

"Baby, this is my cop friend Bernard, Bernard this is my... my..."

"Her fiancé." Blessing replied then eyed me. I looked at him like he had lost his everlasting mind because this nigga hadn't even made me his girlfriend.

"Well I came to...ummm. I came to tell you that Paul was released from prison." he said nervously.

"Yeah, I got a call but I didn't know it would be this soon."

"Yeah, he was released early. Well you take care and call me."

"Okay, I will do and thank you so much." I told him then turned to Blessing.

"Call that nigga my ass." Blessing said getting into the car. He pulled off from the curb all while he wore this look I couldn't read. *This nigga jealous.* I smiled to myself. It was actually kind of cute how a man of his caliber could be jealous of someone like me. I guess I did underestimate myself too much. I laid back in my seat and began playing around on my phone. I had downloaded Family Feud so I was gonna busy myself with that.

When we pulled up to the hotel, it wasn't nothing like I imagined. I thought he was gonna have us in a decent motel but instead we were staying inside the Royal Hotel on Bourbon Street. The hotel was nice as hell and I reluctantly got out of the car knowing it cost a lot. I had heard of the hotel and it was very expensive. Now don't get me wrong, I was used to nice things.

My parents had money and Paul had a legitimate company that was left to him from his father. He was very wealthy and even handsome; the man just had mental issues that I guess he eventually took out on me.

"I'll have somebody bring y'all stuff up so don't trip." he grabbed Miracle's hand and we headed inside. I guess he had already checked in and paid because we walked right to the elevator and headed upstairs. When we walked into the room, there was two separate rooms that were conjoined. It had a jacuzzi bathtub and even a small kitchen. As I examined the room I noticed Blessing hadn't got comfortable so I took it as he was gonna leave. A part of me became jealous because I figured he was gonna run home to his girlfriend that he swore he don't care about. He reached into his pocket and pulled out a wad of money. Peeling off eight one hundred dollar bills he dropped it on the counter and headed for the door.

"Are you coming back." I bit my bottom lip nervously. I wasn't scared of Blessing. I was scared of the things that came out his mouth. Ever since I was a child my feelings got hurt easily and until this day nothing had changed. I was still very sensitive and with the things I had been through in the last three years, I was very emotional as well.

"Should I come back?" he replied flatly.

"I mean, yeah." again I bit my bottom lip. He didn't say anything this time. Instead, he hit me with a look like he didn't believe I wanted him to come back. He walked out the door and I couldn't help it. I followed behind him and watched his figure breeze down the hall. I was hoping he would at least turn around but he never did. Instead, he hopped right on the elevator leaving me feeling foolish. I closed the door and sighed out frustrated. I was gonna get Miracle settled then send his ass a long text.

CHAPTER 13

Blessing

*My Peace: You told me I was your peace but it
sure don't seem like it.*

*My Peace: You demand I leave the shelter just to
drop me off and turn your back on me.
I was fine where I was shit!*

My Peace: I guess I was your pity party.

*My Peace: whatever I did to you I'm sorry.
I'll leave you alone because clearly this ain't what you want. Nice
life and thanks for the room.*

I read the same four texts over and over that had come from
Cherish two nights ago. Right now I wasn't fucking with her
because I was damn near gonna snap. Just her talking to that
cop nigga had me hot. Not to mention, whoever the fuck this
Paul nigga was they discussed. I wanted so bad to submit to her
but I couldn't because I was capable of anything. I know I might
be jumping to conclusions but I couldn't help the shit. It didn't
help Thanksgiving was getting closer and closer. I felt bad for
leaving her hanging, but I had fell into a dark space that I had
to deal with alone. Just in these two days, I torched four people.
The cop and Paul were next on my list.

I been in this dungeon for two straight days. I hadn't answered my phone which was the reason there was banging at the door. Finally moving, I dragged myself to the door. I knew it wouldn't be anybody but Echo or Shani because they were the only two that knew where to find me.

"You good?" Shani eyed me with so much emotion. She knew how I was when I got like this. I nodded my head yes and she walked in and took a seat beside the fire. I went to my normal seat and sat beside her. We both looked into the fire and didn't say a word. There was a silence for at least twenty minutes before I finally spoke.

"You talk to her?"

"Yeah. She's upset right now." I didn't reply. I just looked back into the flames. "You gotta stop doing her like that Bless. I know you like her and sooner or later you're gonna lose her before you even make shit official. That girl cried to me." When she said that my neck almost snapped. I couldn't believe what she said because Cherish always played so tough. "Miracle keeps asking for you too. Something about you promised to take her to pizza. Was all she kept saying. You should go see her. While you and Miracle at the pizza place I'll take Cherish to the spa. Then I'll take Miracle home with me." I nodded my head yes. What else was there to say? My cousin was right; if I didn't get my shit together I would lose Cherish. I hadn't even gotten rid of Meka so I could work shit out with Cherish and already I was fucking up.

"Thanksgiving is a week away." she looked at me nervously. "I think you and Cherish should come eat dinner Blessing. Especially because the shit she's been through you can't just steal her joy. Not to mention, Miracle; that girl is excited about the day. She mentioned eating turkey." I didn't say shit because I seriously doubted celebrating. I didn't mind if Cherish went to my family's house, however, I was gonna lock myself away in my torch like I did every year.

Shani had sat here with me for damn near the whole night. She talked, I listened as we watched the flames like we were at a campfire. Anytime she found me here, she wouldn't leave my side. I guess she was worried about me and I didn't blame her. When I was in this state, I was capable of anything. Hell, thoughts of torching Meka had even crossed my mind so I could be with Cherish. The only scary part about being with Cherish was, could she deal with me like this? Could she accept my life-style? See, Meka was already trained. She didn't know one hundred percent what I did but she knew not to bother me when I got like this. She also had become accustomed to my lifestyle so she knew how I moved. I wasn't used to answering to no one. Which was the reason Meka had her own place. I didn't want to let Cherish down like I was doing now but once again can she handle me at my worst? This shit wasn't intentional, I was just the type of nigga that needed space. But after talking to Shani, I was gonna wake up tomorrow, eat a good breakfast and go with her plans. I was gonna spend time with Miracle then give Cher-ish my undivided attention.

***

The next day I woke up feeling much better thanks to Shani. We ended up leaving the torch at five this morning so all I had time to do was come home to get dressed. I knew if I went to sleep I would sleep the entire day away so I chose to sleep later. I had a date with Cherish that she knew nothing about. I had just got done sliding on my clothes so I was about to head out to get Miracle. After locking up the house, I hopped into the whip and headed for the spa Shani owned. On the way, I stopped and grabbed Cherish two dozens of red and white roses. I couldn't believe I was doing this because I never bought a chick flowers. I even signed the card.

To My Peace,
Don't give up on me.

When I pulled up to the spa, I grabbed the roses from my passenger seat then headed inside. The first person I spotted was

Miracle who ran up to me and jumped into my arms. Shit made me feel hella good. It's like Miracle loved a nigga more than her mommy. She was always excited to see me no matter how much I was letting her down.

I looked over to the spa table and locked eyes with Cherish. She looked surprised to see me which told me Shani hadn't told her our plans. Instead of focusing on Cherish, I took a knee in front of Miracle. I pulled a single rose from the stack..

"Miracle, I'm sorry lil ma. I know I've been promising you pizza. Would you accept my apology?" her little self didn't bother to reply. Instead, she smiled and began chewing on her finger. I pulled her into me for a hug and she began giggling. I then handed her the rose and stood up. Now it was time to face Cherish who watched everything from across the room. I grabbed Miracle by the hand and pulled her with me towards Cherish. When I made to her, she sat straight up. I handed her the roses but she was pulling that tough shit. I could tell she was excited but she had to act unmoved because she wanted to show me she was mad.

"Thank you." she said and sat the roses on the side of her.

"If you don't mind I'mma take Cherish to get pizza. Once we done Shani gonna take her to her crib with her so we can go back to the room.

"Okay." she replied shocking me even more. I just knew she was about to talk shit. I pulled her face into my hand and for the first time I kissed her.

"Ummm." a soft moan escaped her mouth. When I pulled back her eyes were still closed.

"I'll see you in a minute." I had to get away from her before I raped her ass on this table.

"Okay." she replied and brushed her hair behind her ear. I couldn't take my eyes off her so I stood there and neither of us spoke.

"Come on Blessing." Miracle said bringing me out my infatuated daze with her mother. Cherish and I both laughed. One last look at her, I turned to grab Miracle's hand. We walked out the spa and I couldn't wait to get back. *Sorry Miracle but we gotta make this quick baby.* I thought imagining what I was gonna do to her mother when I got back.

***

On our way to Shani's, Miracle was in the backseat knocked out. I pulled my phone out because Meka had called me three times. The last time I had seen her was the night I had to torch that fat nigga for disrespecting Cherish and Shani. That was four days ago and she had been blowing me up ever since. Since the night at my parents' house, we haven't discussed what had happened. To be honest, I didn't have shit to say about that day. Like I said before, Meka didn't run me and if she was that mad she could leave a nigga.

"So, you finally decide to call after four days?"

"What's up Meka?"

"Nigga, you know what's up. That shit pulled at your fam house was foul as fuck. You basically disrespected me in front of everybody. Then, you say fuck me and don't come home for four days. All the times you've cheated you've never did me like this for no bitch. What is it about her? Is this bitch one of your many flings or are you really falling for her? Let me know Blessing."

"That's my friend." I told her honestly. I hadn't gave Cherish a title so this what I was running with; for now.

"Your friend? Nigga are you fucking serious. So what about me? What about yo bitch at home?" her voice cracked as if she was gonna start crying.

"Meka, I ain't got no bitch at home. You my girl but you got yo own crib so please stop acting like we some married happy couple that lives together."

"I thought we had something." she sobbed into the phone.

"We did...I mean we do."

"Wowww. So have you fucked her?" she wept as she waited my reply.

"No. it's not like that...."

Before I could finish my sentence, Miracle had woke up whining.

"My tummy hurt." she whined rubbing her stomach.

"Who the fuck is that?" Meka asked.

"I'mma call you back." I hung up before she could say another word. Miracle had sat completely up and was holding her stomach with a frown.

"You gotta boo boo girl." I told her and she laughed. "You ate too much pizza." I laughed with her. This girl had ate an entire medium pizza to herself so of course her stomach was aching. Shit, I ate a whole large one and my stomach felt like it was gonna bust.

I put the pedal to the medal before Miracle ended up with the bubble guts. I knew how that shit felt so I was trying to get her there; and fast.

CHAPTER 14

Cherish

I had the most relaxing day today, something I hadn't had in years. Miracle had went with Blessing and Shani had a massage and facial set up for me inside her spa. The way my body was feeling thanks to Blessing, I really needed that massage. Right now, I laid on Shani's sofa watching Jason's Lyric. The sound of Shani's front door opening made my heart beat. Miracle came in rubbing her stomach and Blessing was close behind.

"What's wrong baby?" I extended my arms for Miracle to run to me.

"My tummy hurt." she said and laid her head on my shoulder. I rubbed her stomach and it was hard as a rock.

"You ate too much." I laughed as I rubbed her.

"Her greedy ass ate a whole medium pizza." Blessing laughed.

"Oh my God you let her eat that much."

"What was I supposed to do? Tell her no?"

"Yes." I replied and stood to my feet.

"You bout ready?" he asked then looked down to his phone.

"Yeah, let me bathe her real quick."

"Aight." he said then took a seat where I had been sitting. I grabbed Miracle's hand and headed into the restroom. I ran the water and put her in to begin bathing her.

After putting Miracle's pajamas on her, I laid her in the guest bed next to Shani's room. Shani was in her room watching a movie after taking a shower. I stuck my head in the door and she was laying across the foot of her bed.

"Miracle is bathed and in the bed."

"Okay. You enjoy yourself." she smirked. I playfully rolled my eyes at her and walked out the door. I went into the living room and Bless was busy texting in his phone. When he saw I was ready, he got up and we headed out the door. I was a bit nervous because I didn't know what he had planned. However, I hoped it involved sex. A bitch was long overdue. And if anybody deserved it, it was Blessing. He had done so much for me I owed him my life.

When we pulled up to the hotel, I sat my roses on the countertop then got comfortable. I plugged my new iPhone up to the Bluetooth speakers and pushed play on my Beyoncé Pandora. Blessing didn't seem like the type of guy to listen to slow songs but I didn't care. I was gonna make the moment romantic. Blessing kicked his shoes off followed by his shirt. *Lord have mercy on my panties.* I thought eyeing his perfectly sculpted body. His body was aligned with nice artwork that covered his chest, stomach, arms and up to his neck. My eyes fell onto the long scar that went down the middle of his stomach. Although he had tattoos that covered, his scar his was still visible.

"What happened?" I asked him scooting to the foot of the bed. I ran my hand down the scar then looked up into his face.

"Happened when I was a kid."

"Mind sharing?" I asked him and he nodded his head no.

"Blessing, you can talk to me. I don't know if you see, but I'm here for you. I'm your peace remember. I want you to talk to me about what's troubling you so I can bring you the peace you need." I spoke sincerely. It was time he opened up to me. I could tell he had so much bottled inside of him and because of this scar, I now knew something disturbs him from his childhood.

81

"Who is Paul?" he asked switching subjects.

"Paul?" I sighed out and laid back on the bed. He laid beside me and I told him everything about Paul, from when I first met him up until the abuse at the hotel. By the time I was done, I had a million tears pouring from my eyes. He hadn't said a word during the entire story. In fact, his eyes had basically went black on me and he looked like the devil. After telling him the story, I was glad to have gotten it out. He now had more understanding as to why I lived in the shelter.

"Blessing?" I called his name but he didn't respond. "Baby." I said and he turned to look at me. "It's okay. I'm okay." I told him and kissed his lips. When I looked at him again, his face had softened. I rolled onto my stomach and climbed on top of him. He looked up at me in a more lustful stare. I began kissing him again then went down to his neck. From underneath me, I could feel his dicking growing in his pants. I took it further and pulled his pants off for him. When he didn't object, I slid his Polo briefs off and tossed them across the room. My eyes moved up to his manhood and Lord. It stood straight up and was beautiful. It was a pretty brown and so thick his veins popped out. I bit my bottom lip nervously. I talked all that shit but I was now scared to death.

"Nah. you pulled him out don't back down now." he told me and flipped me over on my back so he was now on top. He moved down to my love box and began licking it so it could get wet. Once it was wet to his liking he moved back up and kissed my lips. He then leaned up on his knees and pulled my body down to him. He grabbed a pillow and placed it under my lower back to give me leverage.

I found the truth beneath your lies
And true love never has to hide
Trade your broken wings for mine
I've seen your scars and kissed your crimes

Beyoncé sang through the Bluetooth as Blessing slid inside of me. I gasped as my body intertwined with his. He was hurting me and hasn't been in five seconds but I was gonna be a big girl. Stroking me slowly for a few moments he began to howl like he fell into heaven's gates. The feeling went from pain to pleasure so I opened my legs a little wider giving him full entrance.

"This gonna be mines forever Cherish?" he panted.

"Ughh yessss." I moaned in bliss. This shit feel sooo good tears began to pour from my eyes. He was gentle with my body as he slid in and out to the beat of Bey. Just listening to the lyrics and the way Blessing was sexing me had my emotions all over the place.

My love was stronger than your pride
Beyond your darkness I'm your light
You get deep you touch my mind
Baptize your tears and dry your eyes

I closed my eyes as I envisioned myself in the video.

"Cherish, you gotta be my peace baby. I need you to be my peace." he spoke into my ear softly. Instead of replying, I began kissing him. I slid my tongue into his mouth then tugged at his bottom lip. He leaned up once again on his knees and pulled my feet into the palm of his hands. He looked me in my eyes and I matched his intense stare down. Not once did he miss a beat as he watched me lovingly. He was still wearing his chain and it moved with every stroke. Something in his eyes told me he needed me. It was like he was pleading for me to be his peace.

"Ohhhh shit, I'm about nut...baby it's coming..." I began to pant.

"Let it out ma." he said then began to massage my clitoris. My legs began to shake and suddenly I could feel my liquid cause a puddle underneath us. He pulled from inside of me then tugged at my arm to lift up. When I stood to my feet, I felt my knees buckle. He pulled me towards the double sided sink and turned me around. Without wasting time, he spread my ass cheeks apart and slid back inside of me. As he began to dive into me, I watched him as he watched himself in the mirror. My ass clapped against his thighs because he had picked up his pace. I squeezed my muscles as hard as I could until I felt myself lock his tool into my womb. The feeling must have felt great because he looked down to my opening as if he couldn't believe the feeling.

"Shittt, Cherish! You trying to make a nigga cumm." he hissed and that's all I needed to hear. I began throwing my ass back as I held onto the sink with both hands. I matched his rhythm. He began to bite down on his bottom lip just as his dick began to pulsate.

"Fuckkk baby....shitttt." he went faster and faster with each word. Then he let out a loud growl that told me he was nutting. As he emptied every last drop inside of me, I threw my ass in a circle slowly. It felt like his legs was gonna give out so he laid his body on top of mines. I let him catch his breath for a few moments then I led him to the bed. Once he laid down, I headed into the restroom and grabbed two washcloth. I wet them both with hot water then went to his side of the bed. I used one towel to wipe his face and the other to wash my juices off him. Once I was done, I cleaned myself up then went to lay down beside him. My legs were weak, my heart raced but all and all, I was on cloud beyond nine. I was literally floating and if I didn't love this man before, I loved him now.

CHAPTER 15

Blessing

"I woke up out my sleep to the sound of my moms screaming. The scream wasn't like a normal scream; it was like a horrifying scream that let me know something was wrong. I got out my bed and went to her room. I was a young nigga so I was scared to death. But no matter how scared I was, my moms needed me. When I got to her door, I could hear fighting and tussling so I peeked my head in. She was holding her face and crying. I guess the nigga heard me because he turned around and charged at me. I wanted to run but I couldn't just leave my moms."

I had to pause because the thoughts played in my mind. I looked at Cherish and she had tears in her eyes. "He pulled out his strap and shot me." I told her and she looked down to my scar. I nodded my head so she would know that's where the scar came from. "My moms came out the room and attacked him. By this time, I was on the ground shot. I was weak but I was still worried about my mother. Before I knew it, the nigga scooped her up over his shoulder and walked out the door. I tried to stand but I was weak. Finally using all the strength I had I slid myself to the door and all I could hear were my mother's screams then the sound of burning rubber. That nigga had took my moms." I shook my head and a few tears slipped from my eyes. Cherish was now balling her eyes out but she let me finish. " It's been 13 years. We put out missing reports, everything and still nothing." I dropped my head.

"Do you think she's still alive?" she asked remorseful.

"For a long time, something in my heart told me she was still alive. About a year ago, I came to terms with myself that she has to be dead and maybe buried somewhere. I mean, how could she be alive all this time and not escape. I know she didn't just give up on me because my moms loved me to death. I was her only child and because my pops worked so much it was always just me and her.

We did everything together. My moms couldn't even shit in peace; I was right at the door." I said and let out a chuckle. Cherish chuckled with me but she was still crying. "So this the reason I hate Thanksgiving." Again, I dropped my head. "The day before, I had went with her to buy all the shit to cook. On Thanksgiving day, my pops had to work so I stayed in the house and helped her cook. We ate dinner, just the two of us and just watched movies. Before I knew it, I was on the couch knocked out. She woke me up to go get in my bed and that's the last thing I remember."

"Now I understand why you hate the day so much. I'm so sorry this happened to you Blessing. Now I can't take your mother's place, but I'm here for you. I wanna be your peace if you let me into your world." she grabbed my hands and looked me in the eyes.

"Thank you." I nodded my head to her and placed a kiss on her forehead. As bad as telling this story felt, I felt a sense of relief getting it out. The emotions Cherish showed as I told her the story let me know she really cared for a nigga. I could remember telling Meka bits and pieces of the story and she sat there unmoved. The only thing she had to say was *damn.* Just seeing Cherish cry out for me, had helped me make up my mind. I was gonna shake Meka and let Cherish be the peace I needed.

"I'mma make you fall in love with me watch." I told her and grabbed her cute little nose.

"I already am.' she replied catching me off guard. That's all I needed to hear. I motioned for her to come to me and when she

86

did I guided her down on my dick.

"Ride that muthfucka." I told her and closed my eyes. Her pussy was so damn good I for sure had to make her mines. I couldn't let her give this loving to nobody else. Now I knew she was loving a nigga, but I was gonna do everything in my power to love her back.

***

"Man, hurry yo ass up. I got my girl in the car."

"Yo girl?" Nigga, Meka ain't nobody."

"It ain't Meka with yo nosey ass."

"Oh, it's that chick you open for." Echo laughed then handed me the duffle bag full of money. When I walked in he was in the middle of counting it so I stayed behind to wait for him to finish. The entire time I kept looking out the window because Cherish was sitting in the whip.

Grabbing the bag from Echo, I made my way out the door. When I got to the car, this nigga was coming out the door. He ran down the stairs and up to the car.

"Nosey ass nigga." I told him shaking my head.

"How you doing? You must be the one that got my nigga open like Arco gas station." he laughed making Cherish laugh with him.

"Don't laugh with this nigga ma." I told her chuckling on my own.

"I'm Cherish." she extended her hand.

"Cherish!" I screamed her name out.

"What? I'm just being courteous."

"Nah ma. That nigga jack off and don't wash his hands." I laughed making her and Echo laugh out.

"Fuck you nigga. That's you jack-off king." he laughed and walked away from the car.

"I'll be back in a couple days." I told him then pulled off. I needed to get the fuck from this area because the police was hot as fuck over here. Not to mention I had Cherish rolling with me. I couldn't put this girl in harm's way. See, I wasn't like them other niggas that sit in traps all day. I wasn't bout to get caught up in there. The only chances I took was dropping off the work and picking up my bread. Most of the time I made Echo pick it up.

When we pulled up to Commanders, I parked my whip and we headed inside. It was Sunday so it was pretty busy but because it was only Cherish and I we were quickly seated. Taking our seats we picked up our menus and began to browse. Cherish decided on the pecan roasted fish and a glass of wine. As for me, I was gonna get the same thing I always got when I came here. A filet mignon steak and wild white shrimp. I wasn't the type of nigga to try all type of shit. When it came to my food, I was simple. I loved the fuck out some steak so no matter what restaurant I went to I had to have it. Other than steak, pizza would be my next choice.

"Oh, isn't this cute." Cherish and I both looked up. *Shit.* I thought as Meka stood in front of us. She had a bag in her hand so that told me she was leaving. *Damn, only if we had come thirty minutes later.* I thought looking at her. Cherish looked back to her menu unfazed by Meka standing here with her hand on her hip ready to trip.

"Damn, for this to be a *friend,* y'all sure look cozy. She's a special friend you brought here to the same restaurant you know I love. The same restaurant you always bring me too."

"Chill Mek."

"Chill my ass. Why you can't be honest? Huh nigga. Just be honest. You and this bitch together?" she spat. Cherish looked up at her ready to pop off but that's what I wasn't gonna let happen. What type of nigga would I be to be letting my girl fight. The shit was unsexy in my eyes so Meka was gonna be fighting herself.

"Yeah, she my bitch. Is that what you wanna hear? Huh Meka? Well, you heard it. Out the fucking horse's mouth." I jumped up from my seat. I could see the hurt in her eyes but she didn't say shit. She tilted her head to the side and her eyes began to water. Like I said before, I have never shitted on her with a chick. The hurt that was in her eyes, came from knowing I had feelings for Cherish. Especially knowing I had basically just chose up.

"You a foul ass nigga. I been down with you for years and you do me like this?" she began crying. "Fuck you!" she shot then stormed out in a rage. I sat back down in my seat and picked up my menu. Cherish looked at me from hers and she wore this apologetic look she always gave me.

"Cherish, ain't shit to be sorry for. Stop always being so remorseful for shit. That bitch ain't you and that shit right there a wrap. You don't believe me, we going back to your room to get you and Miracle shit. Y'all moving in." I told her and her face dropped.

"I..I..I don't know about that. I mean it's so soon."

"Fuck you mean you don't know?"

"I'm supposed to be getting my apartment soon; what I'mma do with that?"

"Look, if you don't wanna come I understand." I told her then dropped the subject. I tried to be understanding about her wanting to move slow so for now I wasn't gonna press her. But sooner or later she was coming period.

CHAPTER 16

Cherish

I lifted up out of bed and pushed the button to the alarm that was going off. I wanted to snooze so bad, I was tired as hell. After Blessing dropped me off, I stayed up all night and my mind was roaming a mile a minute. I called him over and over but he never answered. I couldn't believe he was upset about me not wanting to move in. I would love to move in with him but I had come so far. I wanted my own place. The way he had kicked Meka to the curb I was a bit nervous. Just thoughts of him doing me the way he did her made me want my place just to be secure. True, I was falling in love with him but how long will it be before he was tired of me. I had went through this with Paul and I wasn't trying to go there with him too. Things were always good in the beginning. Although I genuinely felt Blessing was falling for me, I still couldn't take that chance.

"Come on sweetie." I told Miracle as I grabbed the remote to power off her television.

"I don't wanna go to school today." she whined.

"You have to go baby."

"I don't wanna mommy. I wanna stay with you."

"I thought you wanted to get good attendance award? I'll tell you what, you go to school I'll order us pizza tonight." A small smile crept upon her face and she grabbed my hand. We walked out the hotel room and headed downstairs.

Stepping off the elevator, I walked past the front desk and the receptionist flagged me down.

"Mrs. Love." she waved me over. *Mrs. Love* I thought as I walked over to her.

"Mr. Love wanted me to give you these." she handed me a set of keys. There was two home keys that made me smirk but the third key puzzled me.

"First level A 26." was all she said. I nodded my head and grabbed Miracle's hand.

As we walked into the underground parking, I searched for A 26. When we walked over, I watched curiously. There was a cute burgundy 2018 3 series BMW. I hit the alarm on the key and when it chirped I instantly got emotional.

"Who car mommy?" I heard Miracle's little voice. I was so consumed with my emotions I couldn't even answer her. Blessing was surprising me more and more each day. First the hotel, then the flowers and now this. Not to mention, the keys on the key ring. I had a feeling they belonged to his home. After I dropped Miracle off, I was gonna do a pop-up. I mean that's what it meant to have keys right.

On the drive to Miracle's school, I couldn't control my emotions. This was the nicest thing anyone has ever done for me. When I was with Paul, he never bought me a car. He had plenty cars that I only drove. I never really had anything to call my own except when I lived with my parents. I had a nice little car they had purchased me in high school. Now here it was, only a little over a month and this man has already spoiled me. Last night after we talked, I couldn't hold back the fact I was in love with him. Beside the material things, just him opening up to me about his mother touched me. I could tell talking about his past was hard for him but he still told me the entire story.

I felt so bad for him I cried the entire time. Now I had a clear understanding on why he hated Thanksgiving so much. However, I was gonna be the one to make him love the day. I didn't want him to forget about his mother but I did want him to move on from the pain. Despite the situation with his mother he had a lot to be thankful for. And him giving me the opportunity to be his peace, I was gonna make him see that.

Pulling up to Miracle's school, I parked in the drop-off zone and helped her out the car. She was smiling from ear to ear because I had explained to her we had a new car. My baby was so excited because we wouldn't be dealing with public transportation. Miracle kissed my cheek then took off running. I watched her as she disappeared into the school before I turned to leave. When I went to walk away, something told me look back. I noticed Miracle's Barbie backpack at a standstill. I made my way where she stood. As I got closer, I clutched my mouth with my hand.

"Hello Cherish." Paul smirked grimly.

"Come here Miracle." I told her without taking my eyes off Paul. "What are you doing here?"

"I came to see my daughter, what you mean."

"You can't see her until the court orders it. Stay the fuck away from her." I fumed. I snatched my child and walked towards the car in a hurry. I put her into the back seat and turned to see where Paul was. He came towards me so I quickly ran around to the driver side. Before I could climb in, he grabbed my arm roughly and spent me around.

"Ouchhh."

"Listen here little bitch. Daddy's home and if you think you're gonna keep my daughter away from me, I'll kill you and end up back in jail." I didn't say a word until he released me. I was so damn scared I eased away from him and climbed in. I cracked my window and only looked at him.

"Go to hell." I told him through clenched teeth. I pulled off, tires screeching and left him standing there. When I looked into my rearview mirror, he was still standing in the same spot. He lifted his hand and waved at the tail of my car. The way he was smiling was creepy as hell and it made me more scared than I was.

"You don't love Daddy anymore?" Miracle asked with a sad face. I really didn't know how to answer her without hurting her feelings. It had been three years since she'd seen or heard from him so I know she was shocked to see him. The only thing Paul cared about was Miracle and she loved him back. However, he was dangerous and the way he had done me I was surprised she wasn't tainted by him.

"Miracle you wanna see Blessing?"

"Ohh yeah. We going to his house?"

"Yes baby." I told her as I pulled over and began rambling through the glove box. I pulled out the registration information and studied the address on it. I didn't know if this was his home but I was gonna take my chances. I jumped on the highway and headed towards the address.

***

Two hours later we had finally arrived to the address. I was sure this was Blessing's home now because of the upscale neighborhood. "Arrived." the GPS spoke through the Bluetooth. I was in front of a huge white home that had a spiral driveway aligned with beautiful roses that was evident he had lawn care. The home was lovely so I could imagine what the inside looked like. I pulled my car up and noticed the front door was ajar. I was a bit nervous but I climbed out and then pulled Miracle from the back. We walked to the door and instead of ringing the doorbell I pushed the door open. We walked into the home and stood in the living room. From where we stood I could hear the sound of yelling. I wanted to leave but I stood there and listened.

"Nigga, you leaving me for a homeless hoe!"

"Man, you got yo shit, just go Meka!"

"Nigga, fuck you. I can't believe you; all the shit I did for you!"

"Bitch, what have you done for me?"

"What the fuck you mean? I cook, clean and wash yo dirty ass draws after you fucked the next bitch in em!"

"Man, you sound dumb as fuck. Just get the fuck out before I grab my strap and you leave this bitch in a body bag!"

There was a faint pause.

"I hate you! I hope you rot in hell bitch!"

Meka came speeding down the hall and when she got to me and Miracle she stopped. She was carrying a box and had tears pouring down her face. Hearing footsteps I knew it was Blessing. He was still yelling but when he got to the front room just as Meka did he stopped.

"Good luck with him. I hope he dog yo ass out just like he did me." she spat then headed out the door.

Blessing and I stood there and watched each other without a word.

"Umm...I'm sorry if I caught you at a bad time."

"What I tell you about that shit Cherish. You don't have shit to be sorry about." he spoke then walked up to grab Miracle. He took her into his arms and began raining kisses on her cheeks. "Why you ain't at school?" he asked her. She was too busy giggling she couldn't answer.

"Daddy came today." she said making me quickly look over. He shot her a look then looked at me. When he put her down, he was still watching me for an explanation. He knew the story about Paul and I which was why he looked worried.

"Miracle, go put yo backpack up Lil Ma. There's pizza in the fridge." Just hearing pizza she ran off towards the fridge not even dropping her backpack.

"What that nigga want?"

"He said he wanted to see his daughter. I don't know, Blessing. Already I see he's gonna be a problem."

"Did he do this to you?" he asked grabbing my wrist. I nodded my head yes and just like that, his eyes went black.

"I'mma handle it." was all he said. I knew what that meant

and I instantly became nervous. As much as I hated Paul and wanted him dead, I was worried about Blessing. I didn't want him to end up in jail.

"Please baby I don't want anything to happen to you." I pleaded.

"Look shorty, it ain't shit you can say that's gonna change my mind." he spoke calmly but the way he was looking told me he meant it. I let out a sigh because I knew there was no convincing him to just leave it alone. "This the reason I don't want you living in that room. You don't think it's easy for that nigga to find you ma? He could follow you or anything."

Everything he was saying was the truth. Paul had connections on the inside because of his name thanks to his father. That's how he only walked away with two years and he had nearly killed me. Giving in, I decided to just move my things in with Blessing. I wanted my place but I had to protect my daughter. And with Blessing I felt safe.

CHAPTER 17

Blessing

Thanksgiving Day

"Boy grab that bag of potatoes and help me peel them."
"Man you know I hate peeling potatoes ma."
"Yo fat ass wanna eat."
"Sho do."
"That's fucked up Dad had to work today."
"Boy watch yo muthafucking mouth."
"Girl I got it honest."
"You sure do."
"Man, I can't wait till that turkey done. I love turkey and dress-ing."
"That's why yo tummy so big. Come on, let's put it in the oven."

"Hey." Cherish spoke softly bringing me from my daze. She walked into the living room where I sat with a bottle of Hennessy clutched in my hand. No matter how much I drank it seemed like I couldn't get drunk for shit. Last night, I had got out of bed to go sit in the living room at my countertop. I had been in the same spot since four this morning and it was now nine. I couldn't sleep last night for shit. My mind was talking to me no matter how much I tried to block out the thoughts. The voices kept telling me Torch but every time I looked at Cherish my heart wouldn't let me leave the house. I guess this chick was becoming my peace in a sense.

"How you sleep?"

"I slept great until I turned over and you weren't there." she said and came to take a seat beside me.

"Yeah, you know I got a lot on my mind."

"I know, that's why I didn't bother you." she placed her hand on top of mines. We both sat there in silence. I really didn't know what to say to her. I wasn't used to being in the presence of no one on this day.

Especially because the shit she's been through you can't just steal her joy. Shani's words played over and over in my mind the entire time I sat here.

"If you don't mind, I'm gonna take Cherish down to the shelter." she said breaking the silence.

"For what?"

"Umm..I wanna let her eat and stuff Blessing. I really wanna stay with you but I can't deprive my baby from this day.

Not to mention Miracle, that girl is excited about the day. She mentioned eating turkey.

Again I could vividly hear Shani's voice and she was right. Because of what I was going through didn't mean Cherish nor Miracle had to suffer.

"It's cool, ma. I already told my moms y'all was coming over."

"So you're not coming?"

"Nah." I said then took a swing from the bottle.

"Okay." she said and stood to her feet. When she walked back towards the room, I was glad because I needed to be alone. I was having too many crazy thoughts and if she said one wrong thing I would probably snap.

I got up from the stool and went to lay on the couch. I wanted to try and get some sleep but I couldn't doze off for shit.

"Why are you doing this to me! Please god nooo!" the sound of

my mother's screams played in my head every time I closed my eyes. I couldn't take it anymore. I jumped to my feet and grabbed my keys. I headed out the door and went to my trap to find Echo. When I pulled up, his car was out front so I hopped out and went in.

When I walked in, everyone's eyes was on me. They all looked at me as if they had seen a ghost. They were not used to seeing me on this day so I knew it was shocking to them. Hell, even after Thanksgiving I would spend my days locked away in my crib.

"Aye Echo, I need a favor, let me holla at you." I told him and walked into the kitchen. When he came in, he had a weird look on his face. This nigga hated when I got like this and that was another reason I stayed alone.

"What's up Bless?"

"Aye, I need a favor. Holla at Ana and get me some info on a nigga name Paul Lucas. He just got out of prison so find out where the nigga paroled too."

"Aight." was all he said. Ana was one of his little bitches that worked the front desk at the NO police department. She was our actual ears in the station and all he had to do was keep dicking her down. Most officers wanted to get paid but because he was fucking her and they had history she would do it on the strength of that.

"Get on that asap." I told him then left. Wasn't no need to hang around because the weeks count wasn't in.

I hopped back in my whip and contemplated on saying fuck it and go be with Cherish and Miracle. I knew my step moms and pops would be happy I came but I couldn't do it so instead I headed for the torch.

***

Cherish

After getting Miracle dressed, I went into the restroom and

hopped into the shower. I quickly soaped up, and rinsed off then climbed out. As I stepped out, I dried off then wrapped up in the plush white towel and headed into Blessing's bedroom to get dressed. I removed the towel from my body and began drying my hair. My eyes fell onto the huge, oversized picture of Blessing's mother that hung over his bed. She wore a huge smile and was standing with her back turned but her face faced the camera. She was tall and slender with a pretty smile. Her peanut butter skin tone was a shade lighter than Blessing's and her hair hung long down to the middle of her back. She was a beautiful woman.

I don't know why but looking at the picture sent an electric shock down my body. I had begun to have this eerie feeling out of nowhere. Something in my heart told me she was still alive. I wanted to help Blessing as much as I could in finding her. Whether she was alive or not, I knew it would bring him peace to at least have the closure he needed. All he knew was she had vanished, and I was sure the most that bothered him was the fact that not a trace of her had remained.

I walked over to the dresser and grabbed my phone. I called to the precinct bernard worked at and had the officer transfer me. I waited for the phone to ring several times and finally he answered.

"Hey Bernard; it's Cherish."

"Hey Cherish. Happy Thanksgiving, how you doing? Are you okay?"

"Yes. Yes, I'm fine. I actually needed a favor."

"What can I help you with?"

"Can you get me the story on Kimora Love?"

"Kimora Love, why does that name sound familiar?"

"Thanksgiving."

"That's right. She had went missing. She was kidnapped and her son was shot. Family put out missing reports but we were never able to find her."

"Yes, that's her. Can you give me the full report and articles on this."

"I'll dig up what I can."

"Thank you so much. And Happy Thanksgiving." I smiled.

"You're welcome. You take care Cherish." I hung up the phone and fell into a daze.

"Mommy, let's go." I turned to the sound of Miracle's voice. I looked at Mrs. Love's photo one last time then slid into my jeans. I was gonna go by the precinct to grab the papers from Bernard tomorrow. Today, I was gonna go and enjoy my holiday. I hated Blessing wouldn't be joining us but because I was with his family, it made me feel better.

***

When we pulled up to Blessing's family home, there were a few cars out front. I sent Shani a text to let her know I was out front. I climbed out and grabbed Miracle's hand then headed up the stairs. Miracle was so excited to have come back, her butt kept impatiently twisting the door knob. When Shani came to the door Miracle jumped into her arms as if she hadn't seen her in years.

"Aunty Shani!" she screamed out. Shani kissed her cheek and she slithered from her hold.

"Where you going?" Shani asked her sensing she was trying to get away.

"I'm gonna help Glama cook." she ran off into the house making us both laugh.

"How you?" Shani asked giving me a hug.

"I'm fine I guess." I replied unsure of how I felt.

"He told you huh?" she asked worried. I nodded my head yes and there was nothing else to be said. She pulled me into the house and closed the door. As we walked through the house, I said hello to everyone. As I headed past the den, I stopped to give Mr. Love a hug. He sat in his lazy boy chair and was watching Thursday night football.

"Who's playing?" I asked him looking at the screen.

"Girl, what you know about football?"

"I love football. Oh, and my team playing." I cheered.

"Raiders or Chiefs?"

"Raiders."

"Welcome to the family." he said and playfully extended his arms.

"I hope we kick some ass tonight."

"Yeah, me too. We hurting without Mack but we got this." As soon as I said it, he looked at me shocked. I hit him with a smile then headed out to find Mrs. Love. When I walked in, Meka was walking into the door with Shani's cousin. As soon as she saw me she smacked her lips and walked past me making sure to bump me. I let out a soft sigh because I was gonna let it slide. I didn't wanna bring any drama to their home so I continued over to Mrs. Love.

"Hey sweetheart." she smiled and kissed my cheek.

"Aunty, did you know Cherish and Bless were official now?"

"Huh?" she asked then gestured towards the door.

"Nope, they done. He kicked her ugly ass out." Shani said as if it was nothing.

"Oh hush, be nice." she playfully hit her with the dish towel. She then leaned in and whispered to us. "I knew it was only a matter of time he left that horse."

"Mrs. Love." I called out to her and we all laughed. She smirked as she headed over to the sink.

"Y'all get y'all some drink. And Cherish, don't get too drunk in case you gotta kick some ass." she laughed making Shani and I laugh with her. This lady was too much. I could tell she was already buzzing and by the looks of things she had drank half a bottle of Rum. Shani reached over and grabbed us both some glasses. She went to the fridge and grabbed a bottle of Hennessy. I told her I wanted to watch the game so we went inside the room to join Mr. Love.

CHAPTER 18

Cherish

Thanksgiving Day

After watching the game, Shani and I went outside to finish drinking our liquor and enjoy the holiday. Raiders had won 31-27 so that made me a little happier. However, I was beginning to miss Blessing. I wanted so bad to call him but I was nervous. Shani had called him but he didn't answer. She also explained to me that every year he would lock himself away. Miracle had come outside and asked was he coming a million times and each time I got sad. I pulled out my phone and sent him a text. I was sure he wouldn't respond but I was hoping he would at least read it.

My Future: *hey babe. I was just thinking of you. I hope you're okay. I know this is hard for you but if you just come be with us, not only would I be happy, but I'm sure your family would be too. Miracle keeps asking for you too. Please, come. I love you.*

I shoved my phone back into my purse and focused my attention back on Shani. We began chatting about all types of other stuff. I told her about the incident with Paul and just like her damn cousin she looked like she was ready to kill. There was no denying these two were blood related.

"How come you don't have a boyfriend?" I asked her not meaning to pry but she knew so much of my business, I wanted to get to know hers. Before she answered, she looked out into the night and I could tell there was something bothering her about the subject.

"I had this one boy I really liked back in high school. He was the most popular boy in school. When I say he was fine, girl every bitch in school wanted him. We dated for my tenth grade and eleventh grade year. It was his twelfth so he graduated. Because he didn't ask me to prom, I bought me a really expensive dress and was gonna surprise him. When I got up there, I caught the nigga making out with the captain of the cheer squad." she shook her head then looked down to her drink. "

Now I had already been hearing rumors they were messing around but being young and naive, I believed his lies and brushed it off. I ran out that prom so damn embarrassed. Girl my heels had come off but I kept running. I was like Cinderella running up the street with tears in my eyes. At the time I was living here. So when I came inside, Blessing was the first to see me. Him seeing me like that broke him down."

"So what he do?" I asked eagerly.

"He killed him." she responded as if it was nothing while I sat there with my hand over my mouth.

"Girl, dealing with Blessing, it's a lot you're gonna learn about him. He has a really good heart with a short fuse. Be wise about decisions you make in life because you don't wanna see that other side of him." I looked at her worried. "Nothing to worry about, though, so don't look like that." she said and giggled. "I can tell he really likes you Cherish. As you call it, be his peace. Maybe you could be the one to change him. Never know."

"Food ready." Mrs. Love yelled out just in time. I don't know how much I could listen to about Blessing without thinking he's some type of *Summer of Sam*. It was crazy because Blessing was this untainted boy with a troubled past but to me he was so gentle. He was sincere with the biggest heart.

After washing our hands, Shani and I headed to the dinner table and took our seats. Their cousin and Meka was already sitting there and as soon as we sat down, they began rolling their eyes and smacking their lips. Mrs. Love came in carrying the turkey and of course Miracle was right by her side. She even sat in the chair next to the one she knew Mrs. Love was gonna sit in. Mr. Love had emerged from the room and took his seat so we waited for Mrs. Love so we could say grace.

After saying grace, Mrs. Love began to slice the turkey and make our plates. The room was awkwardly quiet except for Miracle aka talking Tina. As soon as Mrs. Love slid her plate in front of her, she stopped talking. Once everyone had their plates we began to chow down. Every now and then I felt Meka staring at me hard. I was ready to snap. Their cousin was also staring hard and kept rolling her eyes. It was crazy because this girl didn't even know me from a can of paint but because she was cool with Meka she hated me just as much as her.

"Problem with your eyes?" Shani snarled looking at Meka. Meka looked to her, and I could tell she wanted to say something slick but held her tongue.

"You know, I'm tired of you always acting like everybody scared of you." the cousin dropped her fork and looked at Shani. Shani dropped her fork also and all eyes shifted to her.

"Bitch, because you are." Shani challenged.

"Y'all don't start that shit." Mr. Love said looking over the rim of his glasses.

"Nah unc. This bitch got something to say."

"I sure do. You over here defending this bitch and don't even know her. What you know about her other than she a worthless, homeless, homewrecking hoe."

"Says the bitch that fucked her sister man." Shani shot shocking the entire table. "Oh, you think we don't know why you don't wanna live there huh hoe."

"And you mad you can't get no dick." the cousin spat matching Shani's stare.

"Bitch, I get plenty dick. And for the record, you don't know this girl to judge her. I met her and liked her. She's really a nice person but yo evil ass wanna follow behind this hoe."

"She ain't shit." Meka finally spoke up. I looked over at the Loves then to Meka.

"Excuse me, Mr. and Mrs. Love, but bitch you don't know me." I shot ready to tear some shit up. Mr. Love didn't say a word and when Mrs. Love raised her glass that gave me the okay to let it all out. "You not my friend so I don't owe you shit. Yo man came for me and best believe as fine as he was I took the offer. Don't be mad at me because your pussy expired. Y'all talk all that shit about me living in a shelter but y'all don't know my story. And regardless, I still got more class wrapped around my pinky than you bitches do your whole body. I'm gonna be around so you bitches need to get over it." I spat followed by a smirk. I looked from the cousin to Meka who sat three seats away. She was fuming as she watched me.

"Y'all bitches bold now that Blessing ain't here. But if he was...." Shani went to say but it's like a dark cloud hovered over the room. Everyone's body shifted as Blessing walked into the room wearing the most angered look ever.

"You bitches got something to say to my bitch?" he asked looking from Meka to the cousin.

"Humm." Shani said smiling and dancing in her seat.

"Everybody quiet now." Mrs. Love said taking a sip of her glass.

"Stay out this mess." Mr. Love said mugging her.

"No I won't. Since the day Cherish walked in, these girls been trying to tear her down and I'm sick of it. Cherish ignores them and they still fuck with her so they deserve whatever comes to them." Mrs. Love said and shifted in her seat to turn her back to the table.

"That's right Glama." Miracle said and I totally forgot my baby was here. Everyone started laughing except Meka, the cousin and Blessing.

"Get the fuck out my folks' crib yo. And on my mama, if you come back you gone wish you hadn't." he looked at Meka. she slowly lifted up and I could tell she was embarrassed.

"She my friend; how you gone tell her she can't come over here?" the cousin defended.

"Cause I run shit." he said and no one said anything.

"You don't run shit." she rolled her eyes. Blessing looked over at Shani and it was something about the look he gave her that told me it was about to be war.

Without warning, Shani jumped up from her seat and began beating the shit out of the cousin. She started screaming for her uncle. He jumped to his feet and rushed over to get Shani off of her. Finally letting up, the cousin stood to her feet and looked at Blessing. She looked like she wanted to say something but instead she stormed out the room with her hair all over her head.

"I suggest you get the fuck out bitch or you next." Shani looked over at Meka who stood there looking frantic. I wanted to laugh so bad but I didn't because my poor baby looked scared to death. She ran over to Blessing and hid behind him.

"Well, it's nice you could join us son." Mrs. Love stood to her feet with a smirk. She walked into the kitchen and came back holding a bottle of Hennessy. She sat the bottle down along with a glass at the empty seat on the side of me. "Have a seat." she told him. He reluctantly sat down and when he did, I grabbed his hand.

"Thanks for coming Son." Mr. Love beamed. I could tell he was excited to see Bless just as much as I was. It was now just Me, Mr. and Mrs. Love, Shani, Blessing, and my baby. I got up from my seat and made Blessing a plate. When I sat the food down in front of him he nodded his head thanking me. I smiled and took my seat on the side of him. Although it was crazy, this was now the best Thanksgiving ever.

***

After everyone had settled down, we were sitting around the table just enjoying the holiday. I felt so much better that Blessing was now more relaxed. He was actually in tune with us. Every now and then I would catch him zoning out. When he would look and notice me watching him he would faintly smile. His father was trying to keep him distracted so he kept talking to him. He talked about everything from football to Miracle. Whenever Miracle's name was mentioned he would beam. That shit warmed my heart. My baby loved this man as much as her own father.

I went into the kitchen to help Mrs. Love with the dishes. As soon as my feet hit the marble floor my phone alerted me. I pulled it from my purse and my heart fluttered as soon as I read the message.

My Future: I love you!
Me: I love you more baby. I swear I do.
I'm very thankful I met you and thank you for everything.
My Future: thank you for being my peace. :)

Just reading his text made my heart melt. When I walked back into the dining room, he was looking up at me. Suddenly a figure walked in. He was huge and creepy looking. When I looked at Blessing his facial expression changed as he looked at the man.

"Boy, you late for dinner." Mr. Love told the man.

"I was busy." was all he said. His voice was just as creepy. It was something about this man that wasn't sitting well with me. The way he was eyeing me made me head over to Blessing and sit as close to him as I could. It was something awkward about the way he mugged Blessing that made me uncomfortable. This man reminded me of Kane off WWE and I was now ready to go. I sent him a text because I didn't want to be rude. When he replied yes, I was so happy. Shani was still inside the kitchen helping Mrs. Lopez so I headed inside to tell them bye. I couldn't wait to get home and lay my ass down. I wanted to lay in my man's arms and kiss him a million times. I was proud of him and I wanted to show him how much.

CHAPTER 19

Blessing

"**W**ho was that man?" Cherish asked bring me from my thoughts. I had never told her about my weird ass uncle because he wasn't important enough to talk about.

"My uncle."

"He was creepy." she said with her face frowned.

"Yeah that nigga a weirdo ma. I don't fuck with him." I told her. I could tell she wanted to add something but she was scared to speak what was on her mind. "Say what you gotta say." I told her and looked from the road.

"I know that's your uncle but it's something about him Bless. Not only could I tell he hates you but I had this eerie feeling about him. I don't know what it is but I did." she said seriously. I wanted to tell her about his incarceration but I didn't wanna scare her more than she was. Instead, I told her about the time we had the fight and thanks to my dad I didn't kill that nigga. I don't know why, but until this day, I still had that feeling I was gonna kill his ass. When Cherish said she was ready, I was happy because I couldn't stand another second of that nigga.

"He reminds me of Kane from WWE." she said and I burst out laughing. I knew that nigga reminded me of somebody. I just couldn't put my finger on it. The gash in the middle of his head from getting his head bashed in by an iron didn't make it any better. He had got into it with the owner at a boogie joint back in the days and the nigga cracked his ass upside the head splitting his shit in two. God was with that nigga because he had to get stitches from the middle of his head down the front of his forehead. I was like six when this shit happened but I could vividly remember him coming into my grandmother's house with his head wrapped up.

"Thank you for coming." she spoke softly changing the subject.
"I wanted to be with you and Miracle."
She smiled then looked out the window and got lost in her thoughts.

When I had got the text with her asking me to come I was sitting in that damn Torch in a zone. I read the text over twenty times until I finally said fuck it and went. Maybe all this time I never had nobody who I felt genuinely loved me so I knew being in her and Miracle's presence would keep me calm. I'm actually glad I did go because my family was happy as shit. Well, except Poodie and Meka. I shook my head just thinking bout that shit they had done. I was glad I came when I did because I was sure they were gonna press Cherish to the point she got up and beat some ass. But like I said, I couldn't have my baby fighting. The only reason I let Shani fight Poodie was because they were cousins and Poodie deserved it. If it had been any other bitch in the street, I would beat a bitch up before I let Shani fight just as well as Cherish.

When we pulled up to the crib, I climbed out and grabbed Miracle who was knocked out. Cherish grabbed the plates of food my step mom had made us. We walked into the house and I took Miracle to the her now bedroom. Tomorrow I was gonna hit the mall and buy her some toys and get them some clothes. Miracle was on Thanksgiving break for another week so I was gonna take her to the pizza joint too.

After laying her down, I went into the room where Cherish

was and she was preparing to take her shower. Before she got in, she hit the Bluetooth and turned on some music. She wasn't about to play all that girly shit tonight so as soon as she walked out, I switched the station to Meek Mill. I let her get into the shower before I came out my clothes to join her. I didn't shower for two days now so I was gonna scrub my body good and then bend her ass over.

You feel the vibe, it's contagious
Look in your eyes, shit is dangerous
Grateful I had all the patience
I know you going through some changes

I lusted over Cherish body as I nodded my head to Meek Mill's *Dangerous*. I had just finished soaping up and the way she was letting the water sooth her, didn't look like she washing up no time soon. As the water ran all over her body, my dick got hard just watching her. Her frame was small and petite with some nice wide hips. Her ass was plump and round and went perfect with her shape. She also had a nice set of breasts that sat up like she didn't have any children. Her dark brown nipples perked up the moment she noticed me watching her. That was a sign to me when she became horny.

Over the course of time, I had begun to learn Cherish. I could tell when she was horny, nervous and even lying about something. I bit my bottom lip as I took my dick into my hand. I started stroking it as she watched me lustfully. Not being able to contain herself she walked up on me and grabbed it. She began stroking it with the same rhythm I had.

"Give it to me." she mouthed into my mouth as soon as she stepped up on me. She was still holding my dick as she began to kiss me. It was something about the kiss I could tell she loved me. It was one of those passionate kisses like in the movies.

Not being able to hold back, I lifted her up from the front and her thighs straddled my arms. I pinned her against the wall and slid my dick inside of her. She frowned up for a minute until

I got it all the way in. She then wrapped her arms around my neck and that was my cue to dive in. I began stroking her slow because I could tell I was killing her. Not only did I have dick out this world, but her pussy was so tight it felt like she was a virgin. Me and this girl had fucked numerous of times and every time felt like the first time.

"Ooh baby...it feel so goodddd." she cried out. I wanted to tell her I felt the same way but I was too busy concentrating on my stroke. The water was still running over us making her slide easily up and down my dick. "I'm cumming already...ahhh shit I'm cummingggg!" she moaned into my ear then bit her lip. I slowed back down and gave her time to catch her breath. I began kissing her neck. Tired of the water, I stepped out the shower with her still in my hands. I walked her over to the bed and laid her down, but pulling her to the corner edge. I stood back and watched her swollen pussy. I then looked her in the eyes and her eyes begged for me to put it back in. I hoped like hell it's what she wanted because I was about to punish this pussy all night.

***

The next morning, I woke up feeling good. I felt like I was a rejuvenated man and a ton of bricks had been lifted off my shoulders. No matter what, I would still mourn my mother's tragedy, however, I was happy I had Cherish and Miracle to help me cope with it. Although I was feeling much better, I still had some unfinished business at the Torch. Echo had hit me with that info I needed about Miracle's donor. Kidnapping the nigga was a piece of cake. He was staying in a small one bedroom apartment out in Thibodaux. I crept in on the nigga and caught him with his pants down literally. Nigga was in the restroom taking a shit. When he saw me, his eyes bucked. He started crying like a bitch as he screamed out take what you want. Nigga thought I was robbing his ass but little did he know, this shit was much more personal. I put a Chloroform cloth over his mouth and knocked him out instantly. I took him to the torch and left his body there chained up like a slave. I was gonna let his ass starve for a few days before I torched him.

"You wanna roll with us?" I asked Cherish as she walked into the room.

"I would love to but I'm gonna hop on the computer and do some research. Do you mind if I work in your office?"

"You can have that office ma. I don't use that shit." I told her and stood to my feet. I pulled her into me and placed a juicy kiss on her mouth. When I released her, I slapped her on the ass and grabbed my Saints fitted hat. Throwing it on top of my head, I made my way out the door.

"Blessing." Cherish called out to me. I turned around to look at her. "Don't get fucked up." she smirked.

"I must look good." I told her and stepped my leg out so she can check me out. She began giggling making me laugh.

"You all I need baby. I ain't worried bout these other bitches." I told her then headed into the room to get Miracle. When she saw me, she jumped up from the bed and grabbed her backpack. She grabbed my hand and we headed out the door. As soon as we climbed into the car, I buckled her in. When I got in, I looked back to Miracle.

"You ready for some shopping Lil Ma?"

"Are we Christmas shopping?" she asked excited. Damn, I had forgot all about Christmas.

"I'm just taking you shopping right now. But in a couple days we can go Christmas shopping too okay?"

"Well, can we go get a Christmas tree today?" she asked unsure as if she knew I was gonna reject. Christmas was now less than a month away and this was another holiday I hated since my moms was gone. I didn't hate it as much as Thanksgiving but I hated it. It brought back too many memories. No matter how old I had gotten, my mother would always get a tree and buy me gifts. She would even wake me up in the morning to open them; that's if I fell asleep.

"Yeah we can get a tree baby girl." I told Miracle and sighed.

She began dancing in her seat and just seeing her glow made me push my feelings about the day to the back of my mind. After all she's been through and living in that shelter, I felt obligated to do these things for her. Not to mention, she was my seed.

Because I was gonna kill her pops I had to step up to the plate. Even if Cherish and I didn't work out in the future I would always be in Miracle's life.

CHAPTER 20

Cherish

Once Blessing and Miracle left, I finished dressing and headed out the door. Them going out for the day was perfect for everything I needed to do. First, I was gonna head down to the shelter to check my mail. After ,I was gonna go to the precinct and grab the paper work from Bernard. We were close to Christmas so I wanted to hurry and get this done. I needed Blessing to have the closure he needed. I hoped like hell he would be happy because with Blessing you never know sometimes.

I pulled up to the shelter and made my way inside. I was shocked to see Danny not at the door which was good because I didn't want to be bothered with his ass. There was a new security guard who was Caucasian and he actually looked like a real officer. He didn't give me the normal hell Danny gave; he actually let me walk straight in. I went to the front desk to collect my mail then I was gonna find Cherry. I really missed that girl.

"Hello Ms. Hamilton."

"Hey Ms. Gaines. I came to get my mail."

"Sure, let me grab it for you."

"Okay." I patiently waited for her to go into the office. When she came back, she handed me a stack of mail that I was gonna go through once I got home.

"Thank you."

"You're welcome sweetie."

I headed into the main rooms where all the cots were and searched for Cherry. When I spotted her, she was talking to a older lady by the name of Trashon. Trashon looked over at me causing Cherry to look my way. As soon as she laid eyes on me she beamed.

"Cherishhh!" she ran over to me and hugged me.

"Hey you."

"Oh my God, look at you. You're glowing." she giggled.

"Love." I replied simply. "How you doing?"

"I'm doing good. I'm leaving tomorrow."

"You got your place?"

"Yes girl. I went to see it. Oh, my God; it's so nice."

"That wonderful I'm happy for you. Make sure you invite me over."

"I sure will. So what's been going up here?"

"Nothing much. Girl same ol same ol. Danny bitch ass missing. That's been the talk of the shelter."

"Like missing, missing?"

"Yes. His family has been up here talking to the coordinators and they put a missing report out on him."

"Wow, that's crazy." was my only reply. I don't know why but something told me Blessing's name was written all over this.

"I got my date." she said smiling.

"Ohh that's so good." I smiled with her. She had received a date to get custody of her kids. She had lost them in the process of the killing. Her aunt had got custody while she was serving her time but the aunt was a total bitch. She wanted them kids strictly for the check so she was tripping about giving them back to their mother. "Well I came to get my mail. I have to head out. You make sure you give me a call okay."

"Yes. As soon as I get settled in I'mma gonna call you so you can come over."

"Okay. " we hugged again and I headed for my car.

This bitch just don't let up. I thought as I walked past Camille. After the embarrassment Blessing had gave her one would think she would have humbled herself. But instead she was smirking in my direction. Normally I would ignore her, but it was something about that smirk that told me she was up to no good. Since I didn't have to deal with her anymore, I flicked her off and dared her to say one word. The ass whooping I was gonna give Meka had her name written all over it. When the bitch decided to keep quiet, I got into my car and left.

When I pulled up to the precinct, I rushed in to see Bernard. I gave the front desk my name and they paged him down. I took a seat in the lobby and waited patiently for him. By the time he came down, I was so wrapped into my Covet fashion game I hadn't even noticed he was standing there.

"Hey Beautiful." he smiled making me look back. I smiled back and got up from my seat. "Here's everything you asked for." he handed me a ton of papers.

"I really appreciate you."

"Oh, it's my pleasure." he said then there was an awkward silence. Like always, I began to fidget. He was watching me and it was something different about the look in his eyes. He had never came onto me but today, this man was undressing me with his eyes.

"Umm...I have...I have to go." I stumbled over my words. "Thank you again." he nodded and I turned to leave. As I walked out, I could feel his eyes still watching me. When I looked back, he smiled and gave me a head nod. I couldn't wait to get out the door.

By the time I made it back home, it was a little after one pm so I hurried into Blessing's office so I could get things going. I didn't want him to walk in on me, and I was sure him and Miracle would be coming back any minute. I set my mail on one side and the pile of documents next to the computer. I powered on the computer and when it turned on I went to google. I typed in Blessing's mother's name and so much stuff had popped up. Instead of going through google, I began to go through the stack I had got from Bernard.

Looking through the stack, the shit was sickening. There were articles of the complete story, a few with Blessing being rolled out his home on a stretcher. There was a missing person's articles and even detailed articles with the vehicle that had driven away from the scene. First things first, I began to read. I wanted to have a clear understanding of what had happened. I knew this was gonna take some time and I was prepared. I sat back in the office chair Blessing had and began my journey.

***

Hearing the front door open, I quickly jumped to my feet and began scrambling around with the articles. I slid everything into a manila envelope and slid them inside the many books and papers Blessing had under the desk on the shelf.

"Sup ma." Blessing said making me quickly turn around.

"Hey babe." I brushed a strand from my face and walked over to him. As soon as I was in arm's reach, he kissed my cheek making me melt instantly.

"How was it?" I asked walking into the living room.

"Rough." he said as if Miracle had worn him out.

"She must be sleep?" I asked because I didn't see her any-where.

"Girl can't hang for shit." he chuckled. He wasn't lying. Miracle would fall asleep anytime we were in the car.

"I guess this was her idea?" I asked noticing a huge tree that sat in the middle of the floor.

"She begged me for it. Shit going in her room too." he said making me laugh. I wasn't gonna object because this was very big of him, especially with him hating the day.

"What's all that?" I asked as he came back into the house with a ton of bags.

"Some stuff I picked up for you." he replied. I knew the bags that belonged to Miracle because of the store name. But when I saw the Lady's Foot Locker, Neiman Marcus, Saks and Victoria's bags I became excited.

"Thank youuu." I ran over to him and hugged him tight.

"What's that?" he pointed to the mail I had in my hand.

"It's my mail from the shelter." I headed to the countertop to begin flipping through it.

The first piece of mail was my and Miracle's health insurance. The second letter was a letter from the courts and I already had an idea of what is was. As I began reading it, I wanted to cry but I held back because Blessing was standing beside me.

"You good?" he asked making me look over.

"Miracle's dad is trying to file for custody. And trip this, he's trying to file for full custody." I shook my head. And the fucking court date is in two days." I slammed the letter on the counter.

"Can he do that?"

"Well, I'm sure he's gonna try to use the fact that I'm in a shelter to get her. But what he doesn't know is..." I picked up the third letter and it was from the housing authority. I was smiling ear to ear as Blessing watched me wondering what it was. I tore into the envelope eagerly and began ready.

As I began to read, my heart thumped and this time I couldn't hold the tears back. What was supposed to say congratulations, was replaced with termination. My housing was terminated due to fraud. I was sure someone had told them I wasn't living in the shelter. *Camille.* I thought as tears poured down my face. I could hear Blessing on the side of me asking was I okay but I couldn't respond. He grabbed the letter from my hand and began reading it. I dropped to my knees and poured my heart out. I couldn't believe I waited all this time to be denied. I mean, I didn't mind being here with Blessing but I wanted somewhere I can call my own. My feelings were so hurt, I sat in the same spot and cried for nearly an hour. Blessing watched me as if he wanted to help but there was nothing he could do.

CHAPTER 21

Blessing

For the last two days Cherish laid in the bed and cried herself to sleep. She slept all day and would barely eat. She wouldn't even move to take Miracle to school so I did it then went back home to console my baby. A part of me was happy she wasn't getting her place because now she would stay with me forever. Then another part of me felt bad because she was really excited to be moving. I hated I couldn't do shit about it, so I felt like I had let her down. Normally I could use my money to get what I wanted but I didn't know who to contact. Last night she explained to me that Camille was probably behind this so the least I could do is avenge my baby.

"So I guess you and your girl didn't work out." Camille said on the sly.

"Yeah, she wasn't what I expected." I lied.

"So can I get the opportunity you gave her? I mean, I have my own place, I can do more for you than she did," she bragged making me more angrier than I was. It wasn't shit this bitch could do for me but suck my dick. My bread was long. Too long for a bitch to even think she could buy me. However, I had to play this shit off.

"Hell yeah you can. Shit, you pretty as fuck and that fat ass got a nigga wanting to wife you right now." she giggled all cute and shit and I couldn't do shit but shake my head. This bitch was too damn easy.

"So we can go to your crib or you wanna get a room?"

"Yes, let's go to my house." she said eagerly and clasped her hands. I shook my head and told her to put the GPS into her own phone so she wouldn't have to give me directions. I didn't need shit traced back to me, and this dumb ass bitch was to dick thirsty to even pay attention.

***

When we pulled up to Camille's, it was a nice little condo out in Lafayette. As we stepped out the car, I threw my hood on just in case there were cameras. She looked at me but didn't say anything so I guess she figured I was hiding from bitches or something. We headed for the elevator and I noticed she hit the 5th floor. As soon as we stepped off I let her go first to lead the way. We walked to her apartment and she stuck her key in, then pushed the door open for me to step in. When I stepped in it was dark as hell so she turned on the light. I looked around and I couldn't front her shit was nice and neat. It was also decorated nicely in a light peach color mixed with a light blue. When she noticed I was checking her shit out, she smirked. She thought she was doing something but I kept my thoughts to myself. I had a five bedroom the size of a damn mansion. The pool she shared, I had my own. The tennis court she had, I had my own. Shit the car she had bragged so much about on the way, didn't even cost half of what I had copped for Cherish. Once again this bitch thought she was impressing me. But little did she know it took a lot to impress a nigga like me.

"Follow me." she said as she motioned with her finger. I followed her lead and she led me right where I wanted to be. In her bedroom. A part of me wanted to give her some dick but I wasn't gonna give Cherish dick away. However, I was gonna let her suck my dick. "Make yourself at home. She told me and walked over to her dresser drawer. She thought she was slick pulling out her little lingerie. She walked into the restroom and came back within seconds wearing a red see thru dress with the matching thong.

This bitch been at work all day, and ain't even gonna wash her ass. I thought. *She really ain't getting no dick.* I shook my head on the low.

"You like what you see?" she did a fancy little turn and eyed me. I nodded my head yes and laid back on the bed using my elbow to prop me up. I pulled my dick from my pants not wasting anymore time. This bitch wasn't even worth me taking off my clothes. I literally kept my shit on and pulled out my dick threw the hole of my briefs.

As soon as I pulled my dick out, her mouth watered and my shit wasn't even hard. She walked over to me and tooted her ass in the air. I didn't even have to tell her. She grabbed my dick and took it into her mouth. It took her about twenty-five good licks, sucks and slurps to even make my shit rise. When it finally did grow, I told her close her eyes while she sucked my dick and she did just that. I pulled the bottle of Chloroform from my pocket along with the rag.

"That's right bitch suck that muthafucka." I told her and she began going harder. I wanted to say fuck it and bust a nut but I could nut when I got home. I grabbed her head and placed the cloth over her face.

"What are you..." she went to say but I had muffled her sound with the cloth. Before I knew it, she was passed out and her body fell to the ground causing a loud thump. I pulled the black sheet from her bed and put her body inside of it along with some dirty clothes. I balled it up and tossed it over my shoulder. I had already made sure not to touch shit in her crib so I slid my hoodie back on my head and made my way out the door. Once again this shit was a piece of cake. My adrenaline started pumping, just knowing I was about to do some torching. I still had Cherish's sperm donor there and today was the day I was gonna do a two for one special.

***

When I got inside the torch, I quickly tied Camille up and stuck some duct tape over her mouth. She was still asleep so I knew when she woke up she was gonna get the shock of her life. Paul stuck his head from underneath the cover and his eyes grew as he watched me.

"You got a new tenant Paul." I told him and laughed. He didn't say a word. He only watched me as I finished chaining Camille up. "Man you a cold nigga Paul. You know our bitch got that letter with you trying to file custody. As a matter of fact, she's at court as we speak."

"Fuck that bitch. You gone kill me anyway." he said truthfully and he was right. Today was his day. The nigga had suffered enough. In so little time, he had already lost so much weight to where his damn jaws looks sunken in.

"Ummmmm." I looked over and Camille had woke up.

"Camille, nice of you to join us." I told her as I grabbed the foot of the mat Paul was laying on. I slid him over to the torch then turned the valve for it to come on. When the flames came on, I watched them in awe. No matter how many times I did this it was always like the first time. I looked over at Camille and her eyes had nearly bulged from her head. However, Paul laid motionless. I could tell he was contemplating something to say.

"I swear if you let me go I won't bother her anymore. And I'm not going to the authorities. I'll leave the country." he pleaded.

"Nigga you should have thought of all that the first time. Don't y'all know I'm not the nigga to fuck with? Both you piece of shit muthafuckas has caused pain to my baby and y'all know what that mean? When she hurt I hurt. I'm the muthfucka that gotta make her feel better. You try to take her fucking daughter like that shit just the thing to do. You know how hurtful that is for a child to be without their mother?" I asked him and dropped his hanging leg into the pit. He let out a gruesome scream causing Camille to cover her ears.

"And then this bitch right here." I looked over at Camille. "This bitch put fraud on my baby." she began shaking her head no, but that was bullshit. "Oh, you next bitch. Let me get him out the way. I told her then shoved the rest of Paul's body into the pit. Camille's screams blended with Paul's until she was pretty much screaming alone. Paul's screams had muffled as his body jerked back and forth as if he was dancing. I pretty much went black. The sound of Camille's moans brought me from my daze.

"Ummmm." Camille try to speak. I walked over to her and pulled the tape from her mouth.

"Got something you wanna say?"

"Please Blessing. I swear it wasn't me. It was Amy." she began sobbing again.

"Bitch, do I look stupid to you?"

"I swear on my sick mother it was Amy."

I shook my head disgusted. This bitch had just lied on her sick mother.

"Damn ma. You just blow yo moms up like that." I shook my head. "Camille, Amy got fired because of yo dumb ass, bitch. Oh you didn't think she told me? Who you think was the one paying Amy? Now thanks to you bitch I got another mouth to feed." I told her and dragged her chair to the fire.

"I'm so sorry....I'm sorry. I did it because I was in love with you" she tried to reason.

"So you in love with the devil," I told her and again I went black. I grabbed her fragile body and went to toss it into the pit.

"Blessing noooo." I turned around to Cherish's voice and was stopped in my tracks. She tilted her head to the side and her eyes pleaded for me to stop but it was too late. I was already in that dark place. My mind was already gone. I flipped Camille's chair into the pit and she began screaming louder. Camille's screams didn't bother me; it was Cherish's weeps that was making me see black. I walked over to her and I grabbed at her arm. My mind said throw her in the torch but my heart wouldn't let me do it. "Throw her in fool. She's gonna tell on you." I heard a voice in my

123

head. Her eyes were wide and she looked scared to death. I began shaking my head trying to get the voice to stop but I couldn't. I picked her up off her feet and carried her near the torch.

"Blessing, I'm your peace baby." her voice spoke softly and that was all I needed to hear. I put her on her feet and just looked at her. Her eyes still looked scared but I could tell she wanted me to come back to her. She could tell I was in another place and when she said it again, I snapped back.

"Blessing, I'm your peace." I looked at Cherish one last time, then stormed out of the torch. I climbed into my car and just drove. I didn't want to go home, so instead I drove to Shani's. I couldn't be around Cherish right now so I was gonna go lock myself away for a couple days. Seeing her scared like that, I was sure her ass was gonna leave me but right now I didn't care; I just prayed her ass didn't report me to the police. One thing I never did, was let a witness get away. And because of my love for her, I made a dumb ass decision and let her get away.

CHAPTER 22

Cherish

I t had been three days since I seen or heard from Blessing. I knew he needed some time to himself so I let him be. I had called Shani because something inside of me told me he was there. When she admitted it, I felt a lot better. Just paying attention to their relationship and now understanding what the dark place was she always referred to, I knew she was the only person he confided in.

The day I walked in on Blessing I can't even say I was shocked. I knew deep down there was something going on with him and that day just gave me a better understanding. The typical person would have called the police or left but I couldn't. I loved him and I wanted to show him I wouldn't judge him and that I was in his corner. No lie, I was scared to death. At that moment, I knew my life was over but because of his love for me, he couldn't do it. It's like he realized right then and there I was genuinely his peace.

At first I thought he was cheating on me with Camille. I had went to the shelter to speak with Amy and I saw his car pulling off. When I noticed the figure in the car belonged to a woman, I knew it had to be Camille. I mean who else would he be leaving the shelter with? I followed the vehicle out to Lafayette with tears running down my face the entire time. They parked the vehicle underground but I didn't go down there because I didn't want to alert them. I pulled across the street and just sat there. I was gonna wait for him to come out and I didn't give a fuck if I had to wait all night.

To my surprise, he was only inside about a good forty-five minutes. When his car pulled out the parking structure, I wanted to ram his shit so bad. But instead, I was gonna follow him home and act like nothing ever happened. I was just gonna pack my things and leave his ass.

Instead of him going home, he made a turn for Lincoln. I followed close behind him but I made sure to keep my distance. When he pulled up to what looked like an abandoned building I got slightly nervous. Assuming he was probably doing some type of drug transaction I decided to stay and wait. He climbed out from the car and popped the trunk open. He snatched out a sheet that looked like it was filled with laundry and entered the metal door. I sat in the car for a little over an hour contemplating if I wanted to just go in. I didn't want to embarrass him in front of his homies but I was too damn eager to let him know his ass was caught. Finally making up my mind I climbed out and went inside. And that's when I stumbled upon Blessing and what I now knew was referred to as the *Torch*.

Thanks to Shani, she had explained some things to me so I had a better understanding as to why he always went so black on me. So instead of getting on his last nerves, I let him be. Well until now. It had been three days and I was missing his ass like crazy. Apparently, Miracle was too because she came in and asked for him four times in the last hour.

I pulled out my phone and dialed Shani.

"Hey."

"Hey, how is he?"

"He looks better but he's still out of it. He's been sleep for damn near two days."

"Can you take him the phone?" I asked nervously.

"Yeah, hold on one second." she said so I called Miracle. I was gonna use Miracle to get him home. See me, he would probably cursed me out but my baby, he had a sweet spot for her.

"Not now Cherish." he said as soon as he got on the phone. I scrunched my face. He had actually hurt my feelings.

"Where are you Blessing. It's been tree days." Miracle said counting three on her fingers. There was a faint pause before he spoke.

"Hey baby." he said and I could tell he was smiling. I kinda felt jealous.

"Are you on your way?" she asked him. There was a faint pause again before he answered.

"Yeah baby, I'm on my way."

"Okay." she giggled and handed me the phone. Instead of saying anything to him, I hung up. I went into the office and began to clean up the papers before he came. Once again, I had spent these two days without sleep researching his mother's disappearance. Between this and Blessing, I hadn't slept much.

So far, I had come up with the state the car belonged to because of the license plate of the vehicle. Google wouldn't give me much except the car was registered to someone in Tallahassee. So for now that's all I had but I wasn't gonna stop until I got Blessing his closure. After what I witnessed the other day, it made me wanna figure this shit out more. I knew that dark place he went to had a lot to do with his mother so I wanted it to be over. I wanted him to have a clear mind and live in peace.

***

Laying in bed I was watching an episode of *Wild n Out*. I needed something funny to take my mind off all the things I've been dealing with these last few days. Miracle was in her room, so I was curled up on the bed with a bucket of popcorn. Just as I began to laugh at Nick Cannon who had just done the freestyle battle, I heard Miracle's voice. She was in the room alone and my daughter wasn't a weirdo by far. I got up from the bed and walked down the hall to her room. When I got to the door, she was sitting on her Barbie vanity that Blessing had just bought her. Blessing was laying in her bed and they both looked up at me. Without saying a word, I turned to go back into the room. I laid back down and pretended to be unfazed by him finally coming home.

I focused in on the television but the shit literally watched me. I fell into a daze just thinking about Blessing. I couldn't front if I wanted to. I wanted him to come lay down and rub his fingers through my hair like he did every night. I wanted him to tell me all about what I had witnessed. I didn't wanna walk around and ignore this situation like nothing ever happened. I also wanted to make him understand I was here for him.

"Sup." I heard his voice but I gave him a faint pause before I looked up.

"Hey." I replied watching him closely. There was another faint pause then he walked over to the bed and took a seat. I looked back to the television because I didn't wanna jump right into the situation.

"You love me Cherish?" he asked but didn't look at me. I lifted up and sat Indian-style before replying. I put the television on mute and gave him my undivided attention.

"You wanna know how much I love you?" I asked without replying to his question. "I love you enough to know that something is wrong. I love you enough to stay here through the good, the bad and the ugly. After what I saw the other day, I'm sure you expected me to leave or maybe even call the authorities but I can't Blessing. You know why? Because I love you. Nothing or no one can make me stop loving you. Nothing you can do would make me look at you any different. Under that tainted boy, I see a loving man that I wanna spend the rest of my life with." I told him as the tears slid down my face.

Instead of him replying, he hit me with his signature head nod as if he was contemplating what I was saying. "I apologize about the whole apartment thing. Don't ever think I didn't wanna live here with you because I love being here. I just wanted something I could call my own. I've waited months for that day. I've dealt with all the bullshit that came with living in a shelter. One night my daughter and I slept on the side of the freeway because Danny wouldn't let us in. I also know you had something to do with his disappearing but I'm gon' say less about that situation. Everything you're doing is because you don't wanna see me hurt and I appreciate that. But Blessing you can't keep doing this baby. If something happens to you, I'll die. Not only me, but that little girl in there needs you." I pointed towards Miracle room. We need you." I told him so emotional then began sobbing. He turned around and looked at me for the first time. He pulled me into his arms then ran his fingers through my hair.

"I'm not ever leaving y'all. I'll die before I leave y'all behind. You hear me Cherish?" he spoke seriously. "You hear me ma? I'll fucking die before I ever leave y'all." he spoke then a lone tear slid down his cheek. I watched as his chest heaved up and down and I could tell he meant what he said. This moment right now was so intense, a fresh set of tears rolled down my face. I was staring at a man that most would refer to as a monster or some sort of killer but nah, he was truly a Blessing to earth. He was torn and I now realized why. Not only was it because of his mother, but he suffered from not being able to save her. That's where all his anger came from. And the shit was sad.

He took a seat back on the bed, and laid his head on my lap. For the next few hours Blessing and I sat here lost in our thoughts. He watched me as I rubbed his deep jet black waves. There was nothing else to be said. We were gonna get through this; and together.

CHAPTER 23

Cherish

They can say that I am crazy
For making him my baby
But that's how it's gone be

I had fell into a daze listening to Ciara sing her heart out. The lyrics to the song held so much truth. Just like she sang "I know he won't break my heart" I felt that shit in my soul.

"Bae, you heard me?" I looked up to Blessing standing in the doorway.

"I'm sorry." I turned around and the minute my eyes fell on him I began lusting. He was wearing a Miami Dolphin fitted hat with the jersey to match. On his feet were a pair of Jordan's that had the same colors. He was looking so good I almost told his ass don't leave the house.

"I'm bout to drop Miracle off and go fuck with Echo for few hours."

"Okay, I love you."

"Love you more shorty." he said and walked out.

We were now two weeks away from Christmas so Miracle was on Christmas break. She was gonna go over to her Glama house as she called her. I headed into Miracle's room to remind her to grab her toothbrush but they were already gone. I looked at the tree in the corner and couldn't do anything but shake my head. Poor tree was bald headed with not even Christmas lights on it. Knowing Miracle forgot her toothbrush I was gonna go drop it off to her and grab some decorations.

I walked back into the office and when I looked at the screen it was flashing. It was an ad to a old modern looking museum. What got my attention was when the lady spoke "located in Tallahassee." Knowing google normally gave you ads from your recent searches I brushed it off and began to clean up. Suddenly, all the documents fell from my hand. I bent down to pick them up and came face to face with the article of the old worn down blue 1971 Delta 88. I picked up the article in particular and studied the car. Flashes of Blessing telling me the story played in my mind. When I snapped back to reality I began gathering all the papers and put them in the envelope neatly. I headed into me and Blessing's room and grabbed my jacket and purse. I don't know what made me look up, but I did. Once again it's like his mother's picture was speaking to me. Her eyes were looking dead at me. I nodded my head yes, and headed for the door.

Driving down Canal, I was so lost in thought I almost didn't hear my phone ringing. I looked at the caller ID and when I saw it was Amy I quickly answered. I felt so bad because she had lost her job thanks to me. Well thanks to the bitch Camille but it was all my fault.

"Hey Amy."
"Hey Cherish, how's it going?"
"Pretty good I guess."
"Are you busy? I didn't mean to bug you."
"I'm driving but I'm okay. What's up?"
"I just wanted to thank you and Blessing. The guy from the dealership called me. He gave me the job and I'm getting paid $22 an hour plus commission." she squealed.
"That's great Amy."
"Yeah, I'm so excited. Well, I'm sorry about what happened with your place Cherish."

"It's okay. I guess it wasn't meant."

"Maybe it was fate because now you have a huge home and wonderful man." I could hear her smile through the phone. "Well I'mma let you go. Come by and see me."

"Okay. I'll bring you lunch."

"Okay. Smooches."

"Smooches." we disconnected the line.

Scurrrrr!

The minute I looked up I had to swerve nearly running into a lady pushing a stroller across the street. I smashed on my brakes and took a moment to gather myself. I looked around me and everyone was watching me. When I looked over, I read the neon pink sign. "Psychic," I mouth the words as the sign flashed.

"Honey, would you like a reading." a lady appeared out of nowhere nearly scaring the life out of me.

"No, I'm fine." I replied clutching my heart.

"I'll do it for free." she spoke looking me in my eyes. I was always scared of Psychics but I had a gut feeling I should.

"Okay." I nodded my head and pulled along the curb. When I parked my car, I let out a deep sigh then exited. Just that fast the lady had vanished however, I still went inside.

"Come on, back." the same lady told me and walked me to the back. It was a small house looking building. It was dark inside but the lighting from candles and the neon sign from in the front blinking gave us light. "Take a seat." she said and pulled a deck of cards from inside an armor dresser.

As I took my seat, I guess she could tell I was a bit nervous.

"Don't be scared, Mija. It's life." she said as if it was nothing.

She began spreading the cards on the table and flipped them over one by one. The first card was a gold mine.

"You may not have it now, but you're gonna come across lots of money. So much money that you and your child will be set for the rest of your life." *How do she know I have a child,* I thought as she spoke. She pulled the next card and began reading it. The card was a simple heart with a stem going through it.

"Ju in love. I see a very handsome man in your life. Man loves you, Mija. He will do anything to protect, not only you, but your heart. He stubborn, a ladies' man but he see no woman but you." she said and smiled. I couldn't help but smile just thinking of Blessing. She read off another two cards, one about a career in the future, and the other was about having another child in the future. I laughed that one off and stood to my feet. Although she said it was free, I still went into my purse and pulled out a fifty and handed it to her. She took the money and stuck it into the pocket of her old, worn-down gown. As I went to walk out, she grabbed my arm making me turn to her.

"Mija. I see the numbers 949. I don't know what they mean but it's something. Maybe lottery." she shrugged then let me go. Because of the numbers, I decided to go by the store and play daily three. I left the Psychic office and headed straight there.

***

Walking into the dealership where Amy worked, I regretted coming the moment I laid eyes on Meka. She was at the front desk and, as soon as she saw me, she rolled her eyes. Because of her fear of Blessing, she didn't bother saying a word to me.

"Cherish." I heard Amy squealing.

"Hey Amy. How's it going here?"

"Despite Cruella Deville over there, everything is fine." she said pointing to Meka. I began laughing as we both looked over to Meka. She shot us an angry look as if she knew we were talking about her.

"Fuck her." I told Amy seriously.

"So what brings you here?"

"I need a favor." I told her and began to explain what I needed. She walked me into her now office and told me to have a seat. As she punched on her keyboard, we chit chatted about the shelter. Once she was done, she handed me the papers. I didn't leave right away, because I was tired of being cooped up at home in that damn office. So I decided to chill with Amy for a while. I had spent another three days sitting inside the office researching. Blessing stuck his head in the door every now and again to ask me was I hungry. I know it seemed like I was ignoring him, but I wasn't. I haven't slept, and I had not eaten much because I was too consumed in what I was doing.

For some reason, the numbers 949 was wracking my brain and this is why I was here to talk to Amy. As eager as I was to go back home and look over the forms I decided to treat her to lunch. We both decided on Applebee's which was right down the street. Because she just started her job she wanted to be punctual with her lunch. So Applebee's it was. We headed out to the car and on my way out, I made sure to flick Meka off. She was so mad but the bitch didn't say a word. Amy was laughing. As we walked to the car I began telling her who Meka was. She couldn't believe it. I also informed her that if Meka got on her last nerve she could call me and I would handle it. I guess that's what happens when you become a *Bosses Wife*.

CHAPTER 24

Blessing

A fter picking up my bread I headed for my parents' house for another meeting. I knew this was about feeding the homeless because Christmas was coming up. For the first time, I could admit, I wasn't even pressed by the day. I still didn't care much for the holiday but because Miracle was now with me, she made shit easier for me to cope. However, we still haven't decorated the tree and I was gonna let her mother deal with that.

Speaking of Cherish, I had asked her ass to come but she was too busy like always. I don't know what the hell that girl was up to but ever since I told her it was fine she used the office, that's where she spent all her time. Her ass stayed glued to that computer. She barely ate and it was times I'd have to make her ass come lay down. Lately, she had been gone a lot for hours at a time. I was beginning to think she had hooked up with some nigga on a dating site. I mean, what else could it have been? She was always gone and on the computer. I swear, if I found out, somebody was getting torched. Straight the fuck up.

As I pulled up to my parents' house I parked my car and headed inside. On my way in, Poodie was sitting on the porch. She was on her phone and had a headset in her ears. I walked right past her ass and went to head inside.

"Hey Bless." she said shocking the hell out of me. I hesitantly looked back at her.

"Sup Poodie." I replied then went inside. Either that ass whooping Shani gave her had knocked some sense into her or she was in the holiday spirit. Whatever the case was, I was blown back. Poodie and I hadn't really been cool since she moved in with my parents. Even before, we weren't the best of cousins, but we were still cordial.

Walking into the crib, the smell of greens lingered in the air. My step moms always cooked big meals no matter what day it was. I walked into the kitchen and she was standing over the stove like always.

"Damn woman, you always in the kitchen. Won't you take a break and let one of these heathens cook for you." I wrapped my arms around her waist and placed a kiss on her cheek.

"These muthfuckas been dun burnt my damn house down." she said laughing. "Get you a drink baby." she said pointing to the fridge.

"You always trying to get somebody drunk."

"Drinking is good for the soul."

"And how is that?"

"Because you forget about all the bullshit that happens in your life."

"And what happens when you sober up?"

"Drink some more." she smirked and took a sip of her drink. I fell out laughing because she was indeed crazy.

"Hey son."

"Sup pops." we gave each other a manly hug.

"Where Cherish?" He asked looking behind me as if she would be coming in."

"Shit, she prolly with her nigga she met on the internet." I said shrugging my shoulders.

"Huh?" my step moms asked shocked.

"Shit, all she do is spend time on the computer and now her ass leaving all the time.

"Boy, that child ain't cheating on you."

"And how you know that ma?"

"Because her ass sprung sprung." she laughed making me and dad laugh.

"So I guess you through with that Meka girl." my dad said.

"Yeah, ain't nobody fucking with that bitch. I hated how I did her but the heart wants what it wants and I gotta do what's best to make me happy. Right?" I looked at my step moms because this was her saying.

"Damn right." my step moms said eyeing my pops.

"Let's go in here and have this meeting." my pops said changing the subject.

Just as we walked into the dining area, Shani walked in and Miracle was right behind her.

"Daddyyyy!" she said and jumped into my arms. For the last couple days, she had been calling me daddy and I really didn't mind. Like I said before, I murked her pops so I had to step up to the plate.

"Sup Lil Ma."

"Aunty Shani gave me a massage today. It was bomb." she emphasized making us all chuckle.

"Sup punk?" Shani said hugging me. "Where my girl at?"

"Prolly at the house." I told her not feeling like going into details.

"Hey Shani." Poodie walked into the room. Shani looked from Poodie to me and used her finger to point. I shrugged my shoulders; shit, she was just as shocked as me.

"Come here Poodie." Shani told her. When she walked over, Shani put her hand on her forehead. "Well, she's not running a fever." Shani said and we all laughed. Even Poodie.

We all took a seat around the table once my parents walked into the room. We were waiting for my moms to take her seat because she was setting up the table. As we waited, I pulled out my phone to call Cherish. I hadn't heard from her in a couple hours so I just wanted to make sure she was straight.

"Hey baby." she answered on the second ring.

"Sup ma? Where you at?"

"I'm...umm...I'm on the highway." she stumbled over her words.

"Where you on your way to?"

"Home now." she sighed as if she was frustrated.

"You good?"

"Yeah, I'm fine. I miss you though; are you home?"

"Nah at my parents'. We having the meeting."

"Oh shit. I forgot all about it."

"Is that mommy?" Miracle asked running over to me.

"Yeah, this her. You wanna talk to her?"

"No, I'm helping Glama. Tell her hi for me." she said and ran back into the kitchen.

"Well I'm going home to take a bath. Maybe we can..."

"Bout time. A nigga gone have blue balls fucking with you."

"Oh my God. It's only been a week," she laughed.

"A week too long ma. A nigga need to feel that." I whispered making sure no one heard me. I didn't wanna sound desperate even though I was.

"Okay, well I'll be waiting." she said and we hung up.

"Okay, let's get this meeting going. A nigga got a date with some pussy!" I yelled out making everyone laugh.

"Boy, you just as nasty as yo father."

"TMI ma." I shook my head.

"What, y'all think we don't be getting it on? We old, we ain't dead. Shit I still throw this ass in a circle."

"Ma!" I yelled laughing.

"Ah haha. She a beast too son." my pops boasted and slapped her on the ass. Shani and Poodie burst out into a fit of laughter.

"Daddy, come on. I don't wanna hear that shit." I shook my head.

When my mom was done setting up the table we all took our seat and began the meeting. Moms chimed in every now and then because she was busy making plates. Miracle called herself helping as she went around the table passing out napkins. Everything my mom did she did and that shit was too cute. Miracle made a nigga wanna have a baby now just to see how she would be. I loved Miracle and she was my *now* daughter but I still wouldn't mind having one of my own. Especially by Cherish sexy ass. As pretty as Miracle was, I knew we would make another pretty baby; crazy, but pretty.

***

When I walked into the crib, the house was dimly lit so I figured Cherish was prolly sleep. I took longer than expected because Miracle and I stayed behind to eat. I laid Miracle down in her bed then removed her shoes and jacket. I tucked her in and headed into my room. When I walked in, Cherish was laying on the bed asleep. Slow music played in the background and candles were lit all over the room. She was wearing a sexy pink negligee and her breasts sat up like two nice sized melons. I lusted over her until I couldn't contain myself. I walked over to the bed and grabbed her legs. I slid her down to the edge of the bed and her tired ass didn't even budge. I spread her legs open and went in headfirst. As soon as my tongue touched her clit, her eyes sprung open. She tried to squeeze her legs together but I pushed them right back apart.

"Ummmm." she moaned half asleep. I lifted the bridge of her pussy to get full access to the clit, and I went to work. I had her ass moaning and screaming so loud I had to tell her chill before Miracle heard us. My crib was big as hell but her sounds bounced off the walls leading down the hallway.

"Ohhh, right there. Shittt, right there." she said and that was my cue. I stuck my finger inside her opening and sat it there. I continued to toy with her clit with my tongue. She began rocking her body back and forth and I could feel her legs getting tense.

After about another twenty minutes or so, she bust a fast ass nut all over my face. She was breathing hard as hell and in midstride she had threw the pillow over her face. I got up to go clean up, and when I got back, I told her bend over. Without wasting any time, she tooted that ass in the air with her face down. I climbed onto the bed on my knees and got knee deep inside of her. I don't know why but her pussy felt different. It was wet as hell and much warmer than normal. I began fucking her long and slow then I sped up the pace. The sound of her ass slapped against my thighs was turning a nigga on more. I smacked her ass one good time, then lifted both cheeks. She began screaming how it was in her stomach but I wasn't letting up. She was gonna take this dick. All of it.

Cherish and I went at it for over an hour until I felt the nut building up inside of me. I lifted my head back and focused on the fat nut that was about to come. She was growling and panting like I was killing her but I knew it felt good because she was squeezing her pussy muscles and cumming at the same time. I watched my dick as it went in and out of her. It was covered with white substance from her back to back cumming.

"Ahhhhh, shit." I let out a growl I couldn't hold in. My hot liquid shot inside of her leaving me empty. I began to move slow to make sure it was all out then collapsed on top of her. I laid on her back for about twenty minutes trying to catch my breath. I kissed her over and over on the back of her neck as she just laid there. The feeling was so good I wanted to stay like this forever. I loved this girl and that was on my mama.

CHAPTER 25

Cherish

I woke up at six in the morning well energized. I had went to sleep early waiting on Blessing and when he finally came he hit me with some dope dick that put me right back to bed. Now I was up watching Blessing sleep. I wanted so bad to head inside the office but I was trying to chill out because it was Christmas eve. I sat in one spot for about forty minutes then decided to just go in for about an hour. I couldn't help it. It was like this shit was getting the best of me. For the last week, I had driven out to Tallahassee going to different addresses. But I didn't succeed. The list Amy had given me was all 949 residential addresses. I had visited six so far but I was unsuccessful so I came home frustrated. Since the psychic gave me those numbers my heart was telling me to just try those.

I picked up the papers along with the last four addresses on the list and began googling satellite pictures from fourteen years ago of the homes. The first one showed a few newer cars in the driveway and a older lady standing on the porch. The next home was a white house with a picket fence and you could see two dogs in the yard. I moved on to the third picture and it was a old worn down white house that nearly looked abandoned. I don't know what was it about the home that gave me that same eerie feeling I got when I looked at his mother's picture. I zoomed into the front door and porch but I didn't see anything out of the ordinary. I moved over to the yard and zoomed into the back. The street view wouldn't let me go any further but something caught my attention.

I lifted into the computer as if I couldn't get any closer. I tried to move the mouse but it wouldn't let me. However, the back of a old blue car could be seen. I couldn't see the full car but I got a good shot of the tail. I picked up the article with the picture of the vehicle and held it side by side to the computer. I matched up the tail end of the car and it was identical to the one on google. I moved the street view mouse and zoomed it into the street. I quickly grabbed a ink pen and began writing down the cross streets. I jumped to my feet and rushed into my room. It was now seven-thirty so I had plenty time to get to the residence and attend to my shopping.

I grabbed my jacket and keys and tried my best not to wake Bless. I ran out the room and hopped into my car as quick as I could. I didn't bother turning on the radio because I was in such deep thought. I didn't know what the hell I was gonna say to these people because I was more than sure they had probably moved out by now. I began to think that maybe Blessing's mom just moved away and started a new life so I didn't want to intervene. *I know she didn't just give up on me because my moms loved me to death.* I thought of what Blessing had said. However, if she did, I would just leave in peace and never mention this to him. I knew this would crush him more than he already was but I would simply leave it alone.

About two hours into my drive, I got a incoming call and I knew it was him.

"Where you go so early?

"Good morning babe. I came to do some shopping.

"Oh okay. Well, I'mma take Miracle to get breakfast and then take her to Shani's. I need to get some shopping done too.

"Whaaa, Mr. I hate Christmas doing shopping?" I giggled.

"Yeah, thanks to my daughter who won't let a nigga live, I

ain't got no choice. And her ass just gave me a list of shit she want."

"Well, send me a pic, I'll take care of half of it."

"Nah, it's cool. I got my baby." he replied putting a smile on my face. "But yeah, hurry yo ass up ma. It's Christmas eve." he said making me blush more.

"Okay."

"I love you."

"I love you too ma."

We disconnected the line. *After I do what I'm about to do, you gone love me more.* I thought as I placed the phone on the side of me. I said a silent prayer, praying God would answer my prayers. If I could find out something, then this would be the best Christmas in history.

***

When I pulled up to the address, I parked my car and watched the house unsure of knocking. The house looked creepy as hell as if no one occupied it. I let out a long, deep sigh and climbed out my car. I made my way to the front door and I reluctantly knocked. I waited for a few moments but no one ever came. After waiting for some time, I headed around the back. There wasn't any cars in the yard so I was sure no one was home. I looked through the windows but I couldn't see anything. Just as I was about to leave, I noticed a wooden door to what looked like a basement. Again I was unsure about this, but my body dragged me to the door. I looked around to make sure no one had seen me and when the coast was clear, I tried to open the door but it wouldn't budge.

I stood up and rolled my long sleeve up and bent down on my knees to try again. Finally, the door creaked and it let me open it barely. I used all the strength I had and pried it open completely. I looked down into the basement but I couldn't see anything. I pulled out my phone to use for light and when I noticed a pair of stairs I decided to go down them.

Making it down the stairs I kept my light on to give me light. I moved it around the room and noticed a coffee mug. I knew someone had to come down from time to time because there was a little coffee inside and it didn't have mold. Using my light, I looked around the walls and noticed egg crating along them. *Sound proof.* I thought which was even more weird. Thinking nothing of it, I walked into what appeared to be the living room and the only thing in there was a television and a coffee table that held dozens of porn magazines. The house was creepy as hell but every time I thought of Blessing, I took a step further.

I walked through what appeared to be the kitchen, and I nearly threw up in my hand. It was trashy and the smell of old food lingered in the air. It smelled like the trash hadn't been taken out in forever. I used my hand to cover my nose and I noticed another door. *I swear after this door, I'm leaving. I give up.* I thought because this shit was hella nasty. I walked into the door still covering my nose. I used my free hand to give me light. There was a ashtray and a pack of Marlboros sitting beside it. Once again, the smell in the room had me gagging. This time it smelled like fish and blood mixed. Not being able to take the smell, I quickly turned to leave. Suddenly, the sound of coughing stopped me in my tracks.

I nervously lifted my light and I noticed a female figure laying on a mattress that was on the floor. I used my light to guide me across the female's body and I noticed chains. I moved the light up to follow the chains and I noticed her body chained up so badly it had welts and dried blood spots.

"Hello." I said making the woman turn around. I instantly began crying the moment we were face to face. I used my hand to clutch my mouth so that I wouldn't scream. Tears fell from my eyes a mile a minute as I stared at Kimora; Blessing's mom.

Crack!

I felt something hit me over the head and when my body fell to the ground, everything went black.

***

When I opened my eyes, my head was spinning and my vision was blurred. Trying my hardest to focus, I noticed the figure of a man. Panic began to rush through my body so I opened my eyes fully. I looked from the man who had his back to me, then my eyes fell onto Kimora who looked helpless. She was staring at me with pitiful eyes, and I was sure she didn't understand who I was. I tried to move over to her not caring if this man was dangerous and that's when I noticed I was chained up. I began screaming for dear life, making the man turn around and that's when I came face to face with Kane; Blessing creepy ass uncle.

"I've been waiting for you to wake up." he said in a creepy ass voice. No one can hear you down hear sexy." he stood to his feet. He was holding a porn magazine and a bottle of Vaseline. When he walked over to me, I began sobbing.

"Noooo." I cried as he used his free hand to touch my face. I moved out his touch because even his hands were creepy.

"I know this pussy sweet." he said and shoved his hand up my dress. He stuck his fingers into my pussy then pulled it out to sniff it. He sniffed his fingers like jeeper creeper sniffed that boys clothes on the movie. This shit was sickening. Kimora watched as if she was used to this but I could tell she felt sorry for me.

When he began unbuckling his pants, I began to cry harder. He dropped his pants then spread my legs while holding the magazine in the other. Placing himself at my opening, I began to kick and scream making him drop the magazine.

Smack!

I held my jaw because of the stinging sensation. Before I knew it, he had slapped me again and I literally felt blood fly from my mouth. Now he had two free hands because the magazine and Vaseline were both on the floor. He spread my legs open wide and again he positioned himself at my entrance. I closed my eyes as I sobbed to myself. This sick muthafucka was about to rape me. And not to mention, I was gonna be held captive for many years just as he done Kimora. I began to think about Blessing and more so my daughter. I wished I never had come but it was too late.

I could feel his dick touching my pussy and suddenly...

Wham!

The sound of broken glass could be heard. Kane's body fell to the floor then the sound of gunshots rang off. *Pop! Pop! Pop!* I opened my eyes and Blessing was standing there with his gun in hand and his chest heaving up and down. He sent three shots into his uncle's body without remorse. He then looked at me and I could see the dark in his eyes. He looked exactly the way he looked the day he burned Paul and Camille but only worse. We locked eyes for a moment but I wasn't looking at Blessing. I was staring into the eyes of Satan himself...

"Son?" he turned around to the sound of his mother's voice. He looked as if he had seen a ghost before speaking.

"Ma?" he said then looked back to me. Another fresh set of tears came pouring down my face as he ran over to her side. He didn't even bother to unchain her. He put his forehead onto her forehead and my heart fluttered. He held her neck and dropped down to his knees. He began sobbing like that once fifteen-year-old kid and it was so sad yet joyful at the same time.

CHAPTER 26

Blessing

As I sat here holding my mother in my arms, I cried like I had done fourteen years ago. I was so overwhelmed I hadn't even bothered to take the chains off her. Finally pulling back, I looked between her and Cherish who was also chained up. When Cherish hit me with a faint smile I cried even harder. I didn't give a fuck about crying in front of her like this because the feeling was so surreal. I let go of my mother's face and dropped my head into my hands and sat here shocked as hell. No one said a word.

Finally the sound of Cherish voice, brought me back.

"We have to go." she said making me look up. I ran over to her side and looked at the chains. I didn't know how the fuck I was gonna get them off, but I would do everything in my power to free them.

"His pants son." my mother said then began coughing. I ran over to my uncle's body and began digging through his old Levi jeans. I pulled out the keys and ran over to unchain my mother first. I then ran over to Cherish and unchained her. When they both were free, I kissed them both on the forehead and instructed Cherish to take my mom home. I waited for them to leave then I dragged my uncle's body to the car. He was a big nigga but the way I was feeling, I had Superman strength.

When I got him into the trunk of my car, I drove out to

the only place I had known for so long. On the drive, my mind was running a mile a minute. I couldn't believe that my own father's brother would do such a thing. I knew it was something off about this nigga other than what happened between us years ago. It was something about the way he always looked at me that wasn't right. Here it was, all along this nigga was the one. I began to think back to when all this shit took place; it was something familiar about the man's voice in my home that night. However, the ski mask had muffled his voice. For fourteen muthafucking years this nigga was hiding this shit. He came around my family and even looked me and my father in the eyes each time. I swear I wanted to kill his ass again.

And here I was thinking Cherish was cheating on a nigga. I had called her phone a thousand times to ask her what size Miracle wore and she didn't answer. When she didn't pick up, I went into the room and began going through all the papers she had scattered around the desk. Imagine my surprise when I saw what it was she had been spending all these days doing. I had stumbled up on a piece of paper that had the address written on it and me still thinking the worse, I drove out to the address. When I pulled up, I noticed Cherish's car so I began calling her again. When she didn't answer, I knocked but no one answered. I went around back knowing she was inside because of her car and I don't know what made me, but I headed down to that basement.

I shook my head at just the thought. Just seeing my uncle with his dick out sent that Grand Reaper into my body. What got me was seeing she was chained up. I knew I couldn't shoot first because I was too scared to shoot Cherish so I grabbed the first metal object in sight and hit his ass over the head. Everything after that pretty much went black. The only thing that brought me back to reality was hearing my mother's voice. *"Son."*

When I turned around, I couldn't believe my eyes. It was

her in the flesh. I had to wake myself up from the dream I was having but I realized it wasn't a dream. Just thinking about the shit a nigga cried all the way home. I couldn't even be mad anymore because I was too overwhelmed with joy that I had found my moms. Not to mention the nigga responsible for all this was now about to be torched. It's crazy because I told myself that one day this nigga would meet the fire. However, I didn't expect it to be this way.

***

I dragged my uncle's body from the trunk into the torch. The feeling alone had me excited. This was gonna be the best torch in God's history. I dragged his body inside right over to the pit. I tossed his body inside the fire and I was gonna enjoy the show. I took a seat on the chair right in front of the pit and watched as his body quickly caught flames. Like I always did, I fell into a daze.

The smell of Guerlain began to linger in the air and that scent only belonged to one person; Cherish. Instead of saying a word, she took a seat beside me. When she grabbed my hand, I accepted hers and squeezed it as tight as I could. This meant I'll never let her go and I hope she understood it. We both looked into the fire as we watched my uncle's body burn in hell. We sat here for over two hours both tranquilized by the flames. To my surprise, she hadn't even flinched. For the first time in hours, I looked over at her but my words were caught up. I had so much to say to her I didn't know where to start.

"Let's go home baby. Your mother is waiting for you." she said rubbing my arm. There was pretty much nothing else to be said. I stood to my feet and took her hand into mines. We walked out the torch and headed for our cars. When she climbed into hers, I went to get into mines but I stopped to turn and look at the building. I then went into my trunk and grabbed the two large bottles of gasoline. Cherish didn't move so I knew she was waiting for me. I turned and walked back over to the building and drenched it with the gas. I said a silent prayer and asked God to forgive me for all the sins I've committed inside this place then struck the match tossing it right into the gas. Instantly, the place caught fire and I watched it as it burned. I looked behind me to Cherish who sat in her car and our eyes met. She hit me with the head nod, and that was all I needed to see. I walked over to my car and climbed inside. I was hoping that the fire department wouldn't show up until the building had burned to the ground. It felt like right now at this moment, I had just buried every dark place inside of me. From this day forward, I would live in peace thanks the Cherish. I owed her my life and I was forever in debt to her.

CHAPTER 27

Cherish

Christmas Day

"**M**ommy, wake up. Wake up."
I opened my eyes to find Miracle and Blessing standing over me. They both were smiling from ear to ear so I knew it was over for anymore sleep. I sluggishly got out of bed and told them to give me a minute. I went into the restroom and began brushing my teeth. As soon as the toothbrush hit my tongue I couldn't hold it. I began throwing up in the sink not being able to make it to the toilet. I felt so dizzy that I had to grab the sink and regain myself. As soon as I went to rinse my mouth, it came up again. This time I was able to run to the toilet. I began throwing up everything in my stomach and the shit hurt.

"You good ma?" Blessing said barging into the restroom. I shook my head yes and stood to my feet. He eyed me suspiciously as I made my way to the wash bowl. I cleaned it out with bleach then brushed my teeth. When we walked out, Miracle was already in the living room so we walked down the hallway. When we reached the living room, I was stopped in my tracks. Mrs. Love was seated on the sofa watching Miracle as she opened her gifts. I looked back to Blessing and the dream I thought I was having was indeed real. We took a seat on the sofa to join Mrs. Love and as soon as I sat down, she wrapped her arms around me.

"Merry Christmas." she beamed then brushed my hair from my face. It was crazy because this is something Blessing always did.

"Merry Christmas Kimora." I told her with so much emotion. Just watching her made me think of my own mother. I wanted to reach out to her but the thought of her turning her back on me for Paul was heartbreaking. My mother had completely disowned me because I was young and dumb and in love. It was crazy because when she met my father, she was young and dumb just as I was. She left me for dead and when I tried to reach out to her, she turned her back on me and Miracle and that broke my heart more.

"Ma, we having a baby?" Blessing said bringing me from my thoughts. I looked at him and my face flushed with embarrassment.

"If she's anything like her, she's gonna be something else." she nodded to Miracle making Blessing and I laugh.

Last night when we got home, we ran Mrs. Love a hot bath and let her soak for hours. Once she was done, we fed her some steak, crab and a baked potato I had whipped up. Thinking she would go into the room and get some rest, she surprised the hell out of me and Blessing by coming into the living room and helping Miracle decorate the tree. We sat in the living room all night until about five in the morning which was the reason I was so tired now. Blessing explained to his mother about Mr. Love being married and to my surprise she didn't mind. Today we were going over to the Love residence then after we were going to the shelter. This was the best Christmas yet and it felt great to see Blessing smiling.

***

After we were done dressing, we headed to Mr. Love's home. We didn't tell him about finding Kimora, so this was gonna be a major shock. As soon as we pulled up, I looked at Kimora and I could tell she was nervous. She looked at the home that once belonged to her, and I could tell that memories flashed through her mind. She looked as if she was gonna get emotional, but she held back the tears. As we all exited the car, we headed to the door and Blessing used his key for entrance. We let him walk in first then I followed behind with Miracle on my arm.

"What you all excited about boy?" Mr. Love asked Blessing as he came out the kitchen. The dinner table was filled with pans that they were preparing for the homeless at the shelter. Mr. Love eyed Blessing who was smirking. "Boy, what's wrong with yo goofy ass?" He asked him. Kimora stepped from behind us, and Mr. Love looked as if he had seen a ghost. He didn't say a word. He only looked at Kimora as she smiled shyly. Although she had lost plenty weight she still looked as beautiful as the picture that hung over Blessing's bed.

"It's almost time. We're gonna be...." Mrs. Love walked into the dining area and stopped in her tracks. The plate she was holding slipped from her hands then shattered into pieces. She clutched her mouth and was lost beyond words.

"Hello Elaine." Kimora smiled pleasantly. "It's okay. I know all about you. Welcome to the family," she told Mrs. Love as her eyes began to water. I looked around the room and, not only was I crying, but Mr. Love had a few tears running down his face and so did Blessing.

"But how? Where?" Mr. Love tried to speak but the words wouldn't come out right.

"It's a long story Michael." Kimora said waving her hand as if it was nothing. "It's Christmas; we'll talk about it later." she told Mr. Love who was still shocked. Breaking the ice, Kimora ran over to him and gave him a big hug. After, she ran over to Mrs. Love and did the same.

"I hope y'all ready because a bitch ain't got all day." we all turned around to Shani who had just come through the door. What shocked the hell out of me was Poodie who was behind her as if it was nothing.

"Hey Cherish. Merry...." Poodie went to say shocking the hell out of me. But she was quickly caught in her tracks.

"Aunty!!!" Shani screamed out and tears began to run down her face like a waterfall. She ran over to Kimora not believing her eyes. The entire time Blessing and I stood quiet still overwhelmed ourselves. We all surrounded Kimora and just like last night, tears fell freely from joy. They all hugged again and that was my cue to give my baby some Christmas love. "Merry Christmas baby." I told Blessing and snuggled under his arm. He bent down and kissed my forehead then pulled me back to look me in the eyes.

"I love you Cherish. You don't know what you've done to my life. Not only am I thankful for you, but I'm thankful for what you've done." he dropped to his knees. He pulled out a huge ring and the words "will you be my wife?" flowed from his tongue as if he practiced it a million times. I used my hand to clutch my mouth as a fresh set of tears ran down my face. I shook my head yes before I finally screamed, "YES!" Everyone began clapping and once again this was the best Christmas.

"So I have two Glamas?" Miracle asked counting two on her fingers. Everyone in the room began to laugh like always at this child of mines.

"Yes, you have two Glamas sweetie." Kimora bent down and rubbed Miracle's head. "All Praises goes to Cherish. None of this would be possible without you. Cherish, you've brought me the peace that I've been needing for years." she said and me and Blessing looked at each other and smiled. "I owe you my life my love." she looked at me and her warm smile made me smile back.

"You're so welcome mom." I replied truly. I ran over to her and gave her a hug so tight I nearly squeezed her fragile body to death. "I love all you guys and thank you for making me feel a part of the family."

"We love you too." they all said including Poodie. We all hugged one last time then headed out the door for the shelter.

The entire way, I couldn't take my eyes off my ring. I was proud to say, meet the new Mrs. Love, and I would forever wear the name proudly.

Epilogue
Kimora Love

Elaine and I stood side by side as we carved the turkey and dropped it on each plate. The smiles from the people in this shelter warmed my heart. Everyone that grabbed a plate told me *God Bless You* and little did they know, I was more blessed than I could ever be. The hell that I had been through over these last 14 years was painful. I sat in that room chained up like a prisoner and every day I wanted to die. Several times I tried to commit suicide but I always failed. I tried strangling myself with those chains and even setting myself on fire. Each time, Marshon caught me and he would beat me until I was black and blue. He always told me if I died it would be behind the hands of him.

When I tell y'all that man was the devil himself, I couldn't believe that any human being could be purely that evil. He held me captive for all those years abusing my body and leaving me to lay in my own blood mixed with his semen. He abused my body to the point I was numb. Every day for the first few years I would scream for dear life but I finally gave up realizing my cries couldn't be heard. He had the entire basement sound proofed and even the two windows were pained shut. He fed me every so often and even let me wash up, however, it was all right there in that bed.

Because of his cigarette habit, I began smoking in hopes I would just catch cancer and die. Many of times I would ask him why he did this to me? And he would always say because he hated his own brother. He told me how he was so in love with me back in high school and that shit blew me back. I remembered him vividly being the exact monster he was today. Even in school he was creepy as hell. He also told me when I got with his brother in school I crushed his heart so he vowed to himself that one day he would get me. Shortly after he was sent to jail for rape and I finally felt at ease whenever I was around their family. The moment he was released was the night he showed up to my home. I opened my eyes and there he stood. Although he was wearing a mask, I knew that man from anywhere. *"I told you I would get you."* were his words before he began to assault me. And that's when Blessing came into the room.

When he shot my baby, my heart ached so bad I didn't know what to do. Until this day, I didn't even know if Blessing had made it alive because I had not one source of communication with the outside world. When Cherish showed up that day, I didn't know who she was. I thought she was just another woman that was gonna be abused by Marshon. I figured because I was now older he was done with me. When Blessing showed up, it all registered to whom Cherish was. I hadn't had the talk with them about my missing, but I knew sooner or later I would.

That night, we sat in Blessing's living room enjoying each other as Miracle decorated her tree. Blessing told me about his father remarrying, and I couldn't even be mad. Upon meeting Elaine, her entire aura was genuine. I know this was hard for her but her too I was gonna have a talk with soon. Michael was now a thing of the past and they both had my blessings. So much time had went by, I knew by now he would eventually find love.

"Cherish, here's your mail." a lady walked over to Cherish and brought me from my thoughts. The look in her eyes as she stared at the envelope made me wonder what it could be. She had this look of uncertainty.

"What is it baby?" I asked her walking closer to her.

"It's a letter from an insurance company." she said then opened the envelope. By this time, Blessing had walked over sensing something was wrong.

As Cherish read the letter, tears began to pour from her eyes. Blessing and I both gave her time to process whatever it was. She looked over at us, and the look she wore was gloomy.

"It...It says my mother passed and she had a $500,000 insurance policy that's coming to me because I was the only child." she looked off into the air and she fell into a complete daze. I rubbed her shoulder as Blessing hugged her and gave his condolences.

Just watching the two of them, made me think back to the love Michael and I once shared. I could tell my son loved her and she was the best thing that could ever have happened to this family. Just like I told her, I owed her my life.

That same night, they had explained to me how they found me, and all night I thanked Cherish. I also thanked God for bringing her into his life. I would forever be in debt to her and now that her mother had passed, I was gonna do my best to fill that void.

***

Cherish

I walked into the shelter and looked around at all the Easter decorations. Just standing in here brought back so many memories I always wanted to cry. Today I was here to meet with the staff and conduct a few interviews for new hires. Yes you heard me right, I was now the owner of the same shelter and I had changed the name to *Thank For My Blessing's* Shelter. I hired a few new people and guess who was the head of staff? Cherry. Cherry and I had begun to visit each other frequently. She had gotten custody of her children and this was a blessing of its own. When I told her I had a job for her, she was so excited, and that too made me feel great inside. I also rehired Amy and because she was tired of Meka she left the dealership and came to work for me.

The money I had received from my mother's policy is the money I used to buy the building. Instead of turning it into something else, I chose to keep it as a shelter. The day I received the check I was shocked. I had no idea of my mother's passing and the part that hurt most, was, one day I was hoping we would reunite. I was thankful for the money but I'd give it all back just to have that conversation with her I had been longing for.

For many nights, I cried just thinking about her being gone and not having that closure as to why she hated me so much. Blessing would always tell me it wasn't me she hated; she hated herself and stop stressing his damn baby out. Yes, I was now six months pregnant with a baby boy. Blessing and Miracle was so excited they catered to my every need. Just the thought of having this baby brought so much more life to the family. I couldn't wait.

Blessing and my wedding date was scheduled for this November 22nd which was Thanksgiving day. I was shocked as hell when he chose that date but it really didn't surprise me. I mean, why not make the most painful day of your life into the most beautifulest. Now that he had Kimora, everything about him had changed. Those dark places he often went to were now gone and he kept a smile on his face that lit up the entire state of New Orleans. There wasn't a day that went by Kimora didn't thank me and I constantly told her to just thank God. I know it was awkward for her and Mrs. Love but to my surprise they got along great. They went shopping together and even prepared dinner together whenever we went over.

Being that Kimora had been gone for so long, Blessing decided to let her stay with us. I didn't mind because I had begun to love her like my own mother. We all had been through the worst and it felt good to finally say, we were all burden free. We lived our life in peace and guess what? Blessing even got out the game. Between the money from our shelter and what he had in the bank, we were living great and didn't need for anything. Blessing was also opening up a center for battered women and of course he opened up a business for the men; a barbershop. It was crazy because I always thought back to the psychic reading I had received.

You may not have it now, but you're gonna come across lots of money. So much money that you and your child be set for the rest of your life. Crossed my mind on a regular. Not only that but when she told me about the child I would have in the future, I didn't expect it to be this soon. I had visited that same psychic office and gave that lady a check for ten thousand dollars. The moment I stepped foot in there she remembered me. When she saw my bell, she smiled. She was so grateful for the check she hugged me a million times. If it wasn't for her, I don't think I would have found Kimora. Those numbers she had given me were the last peace to the puzzle. I also introduced the woman to Kimora and they were now besties. She would always come over for dinner or Kimora would spend time at her home. Besides hearing the news about my mother, everything in my life was perfect. And for the first time, Thanksgiving and Christmas were gonna be more than just a holiday. I was so Thankful for the things I had been through because it made me a firm believer that prayers did work. Once again, we all had that *Peace* we all longed for.

The End....

Happy Holidays Everyone!

"This book is dedicated to my G Pops Daniel Danzwel Owens"
Thank you so much for taking the time out to give me ideas. Boy when I tell y'all we sat at my dinner table with Pandora 'Body and Soul' station playing, and bottles of Hennessy. Our brains roamed, we laughed but overall we came up with the best ideas. Thank you again Dad!

Message from the author:
Let me tell y'all how I cried five times off writing this book. My emotions were all over the place and on some parts I was even scared lol "yes I'm still scared of the dark" don't judge me. This book was really an inspiration and I hope I could inspire some of you. Be thankful for the things you have, even if you don't have much because remember, there's always someone doing worse than you.

Thank you to everyone who enjoyed this book. I really appreciate y'all from the bottom of my heart. Once again HAPPY THANKSGIV-ING!!!

Visit My Website
http://authorbarbiescott.com/?v=7516fd43adaa

Barbie Scott Book Trap (Book Club) click below to see character visuals, enter contests and have literary fun with polls.
https://www.facebook.com/groups/1624522544463985/

Like My Page On Facebook
https://www.facebook.com/AuthorBarbieScott/?modal=composer

Instagram:
https://www.instagram.com/authorbarbiescott/?hl=en

CPSIA information can be obtained
at www.ICGtesting.com
Printed in the USA
LVHW111602051120
670844LV00003B/504